Sisterhood

The Story of Bella

Sisterhood

The Story of Bella

KATHY HOUCHINS

ARPress
45 Dan Road Suite 5
Canton MA 02021

Hotline: 1(888) 821-0229
Fax: 1(508) 545-7580

Ordering Information:
Quantity sales. Special discounts are available on quantity purchases by corporations, associations, and others. For details, contact the publisher at the address above.

Printed in the United States of America.

ISBN-13:   Softcover   979-8-89356-627-7
           eBook   979-8-89356-628-4

Library of Congress Control Number: 2024903484

TABLE OF CONTENTS

THE SISTERHOOD BELLA
(BOOK 1)

INTRODUCTION

This book is the first in a series of stories about a group of ladies who would be considered by some to be the "good ole gals" of their community. They controlled a lot of people and how their community worked without anyone really knowing who they were or what they did. The how they maintained control is still not understood but acknowledged by this author who has seen them at work and understands how successful they really were.

Additionally, each story contains a lesson to be learned. Within the Bella story the lesson regarding TRUST is brought forward. A definition of "trust" is *a firm belief in the reliability, truth, ability or strength of someone or something: relations have to be built on trust.*

Back in the day of their parents, women didn't have active roles in any kind of business. They were to stay at home and take care of the family needs. Their list of responsibilities included the household chores of preparing proper meals and laundry maintenance along with any other items that needed attending relating to the running of the house. They were to help their spouses maintain the decorum of the day and to uphold the most respectful attributes of society which included the successful husband and doting wife with perfect children household.

Well, that was not going to be how things worked with this group of ladies. They had all grown up together in a small community in the southland known as Hamp's Bayou, Mississippi which sat about an hour north of the Mississippi Gulf Coast. They had been indoctrinated in the ways of the perfect southern family image. They all understood that the southern image was false for them and they were not going to sit by and allow that impression happen in their lives. The public image was one thing and the reality of what was really going on behind those close doors was something else. The "Leave It To Beaver" household was only meant for television. However, many of the southern traditions were to remain faithfully followed or possibly altered to meet particulars to satisfy them individually.

There were 4 of them in the sisterhood. They were thick as thieves and had each other's back. In those early years they would meet behind the barn at Eleanor's farm whenever they could to catch up with one another and then talk about their dreams and what they would never allow in their lives. This all started somewhere around the 5th grade but nobody can actually recall the first time they met like this. They all remember the swearing in of each member and that they would never let anything or anybody come between them. And that was a "forever" promise. The oath was sworn to and sealed in blood and that was all there was to it.

The girls grew extremely close over those school years. They knew more about each other than their families knew about them individually. They shared all their dreams with one another. Nothing was sacred or taboo to talk about. They knew that no matter what, that each member would be there to support them if there was ever a need for that. When they had to leave for their respective universities, they kept in constant contact with one another as many times they each needed the support from the group. The summertime reunions were fabulous as they had so much to share with each other. They were learning so much about the world and how it worked. How it all panned out was quite interesting.

Eleanor Becks had no choice as to where she was headed as her father was the CEO of the local bank and she was the only child and it was automatically understood that she would have to move up into her father's business. She had a good mind for numbers and had no problem doing this. They all agreed that Eleanor was perfect for the job and they helped keep her focused on that future.

Then there was Isabella "Bella" Donatar. She had a flair for dressing in the latest fashions and they all knew that she would one day be either a model or fashion designer. Bella was more than perfect for the job and started early by entering beauty pageants and she won most that she entered. She loved to write about fashion and to discuss it with anyone who would listen. Yes, her profession was predestined. This book tells a story about this sweet, young woman who has a major, life changing incident happen to her and how the sisters handled it for her. Only a select few knew the real story and now so will you. And the lesson of Trust will be revealed.

Next came Luna Wadsworth. Oh how she hated that last name and vowed that when she was older, she would change it. Anyway, Luna was the thinker. She had the smarts of the group as they liked to tease. Luna was always thinking about how things worked and had a major liking of anything legal. Somehow, they all knew she would be a very powerful and influential attorney.

The fourth member was Evie Tack. This woman had an eye for seeing what the future held as far as expansion of a community. She forecast so many property expansions that most of the group were amazed at her accuracy. In later years, nobody would consider buying any piece of property without contacting Evie and of course Evie was the person to see when they purchased their personal homes and business structures. Evie had her hand in just about every real estate transaction in the entire county and possibly most of Mississippi.

There was an understanding that these girls would grow into fabulous women that would change the world around them and always be there to help each other. That help would manifest itself multiple times and their blood bond kept all the secrets necessary to allow them to continue forward with their lives.

And now the story begins…..

CHAPTER 1

Bella

This is exactly the kind of morning that Bella loved the most. The sky was deep blue with wispy clouds here and there. There was a slight warm breeze brushing against her cheeks as she stepped outside. The early morning robins were signing their happy melody putting a smile on Bella's face. The air was filled with an aroma of lilacs and gardenias. Life just seemed perfect. She stood ever so still, taking in a deep breath, just enjoying the moment. Not many days brought her this type of comfort and joy. The past few months were hell and she was happy to be able to feel this way again.

She was ready to jump in and get her day started. She pushed the garage remote to open the door and she headed towards her car. She opened the car door, got in and strapped on her seat belt. Turning the key on the ignition she listened to the roar of the engine of her new convertible. Once the garage door opened, she pulled out to let the top down. This morning deserved to be experienced fully. Nothing was going to pull her back down again.

She never noticed the dark shadow in the rear corner of the garage that was outlined in the shape of a large man. The shadow seemed to have a smile on its face as the garage door closed with Bella pulling away. Hector reached for his cell phone.

These past few months have been quite a drain on her. There were a few moments when she was not so sure she could endure it all. Thank goodness her sisters were there. She could not have come through it all if it had not been for them. She thankfully recalled how her sisters took care of everything. Yes indeed, they always cared what happened to her and forever had her back. She felt truly blessed to have them in her life.

With the wind blowing through her hair, Bella turned south to take the long way into her office. This morning was just too beautiful not to fully enjoy it. The bright morning sun glistened down on her, putting a glow on her cheeks. The warm wind whipped her hair all around. The roar of the engine made her heart feel every beat. It made her feel free. This felt so wonderful and she realized just how much she missed feeling happy and contented.

Isabella Donatar-Thomas fondly known as Bella was stunning in her beauty and grace all her life. She was born with a full head of dark, almost ebony black hair to her waist and her eyes were an incredible deep blue. Most people would stop and marvel at her natural beauty. As she matured, her body took on a slender yet alluring shape and she stood at 5'10" tall. That was perfect for the fashion industry that would make her famous. When she entered a room, everyone would turn to see who she was.

As she was riding along her cell phone rang and it was her dear sweet friend Eleanor. "Hey Bella, Eleanor here. Care to have lunch today?" said Eleanor in a strong southern drawl that Bella almost giggled out loud.

"To have lunch with you my friend is a real treat. I will clear my schedule. What time and where" …. was her response.

After a few minutes of determining the restaurant, they were set.

"OK, sounds like fun. I will see you there around 12:30…. confirmed Bella and she hung up. Her day was turning out much better than she thought it would.

Bella became friends with Eleanor Beck when they were in the 5th grade. They had attended the same school since 2nd grade, but Bella just could not remember Eleanor any earlier than 5th grade. They had lockers in the hallway that were side by side that year and that is how they met. Once the bond was established, they were inseparable.

Eleanor introduced Bella to her friend Luna Wadsworth who had been Eleanor's friend since 2nd grade. The three of them were always together and became extremely close over those years. Evie Tack joined up with this group later that year and they created the "sisterhood" of Hamp's Bayou.

While driving Bella had a flashback memory of when the sisterhood really learned why they were brought together. How incredible their skills were and how they complimented each other? She had no idea any of this was possible until that time when Evie told her what was going to happen at a party Bella was attending and sure enough it happened exactly like Evie said it would. Her date was a jerk who tried to rape her and Eleanor, Luna and Evie were right there to stop it. Her date learned that you don't fool with the sisterhood. Bella and the others learned that Evie knew what she was talking about.

And thus the sisterhood was formed, skills were honed, respect was established for each member's ability and all were sworn to protect each other when needed. This was their secret and it was not to be shared with anyone else. This was sworn to with a blood oath taken when they were all 16 yrs old. That oath has never been broken.

Bella was the odd woman out as she did not attend a college but rather a modeling school to hone her skills. She had been working all through high school for a local modeling school and had had several contracts for modeling jobs in the area and in New Orleans. The owner of the school could see the potential that Bella had and agreed to help her promote herself in New York and other areas to increase her exposure. Together they put her portfolio together and sent it out to several modeling and fashion houses in New York City.

Bella's big break came when she was offered a modeling job in New York City for a major fashion house when she was 18, during the summer after her high school graduation. Her first hurtle was to tell her parents as they had grown to depend on her taking care of her mother. Secondly, she had to leave the only security she had ever known and that was her comfort in the sisterhood she shared with her 3 best friends. Leaving her "sisters" scared her more than leaving her family.

She was the first to say goodbye to the sisterhood. The day was cloudy and rainy which took on the moods of the sisters as they had to be separated for an unknown time as their individual lives moved forward. They collectively were happy for each other with the prospects each had, but saying goodbye was difficult for them. They promised to keep in touch and to visit as often as possible. Eleanor, Evie, and Luna hugged themselves as they waved goodbye to Bella as she boarded the airplane to New York City. Life was changing and would never again be like it was for them.

Bella arrived in New York City, hailed a cab, and headed immediately to the fashion house that had contacted her about working for them. They had an apartment that she would have to share with another model working for them but it solved her living arrangement dilemma. She was introduced to Sophia, who was from France and spoke broken English who would share the apartment with her. Bella thought that this arrangement was going to be fun. Later she discovered that it would not be as she had hoped but would be a difficult situation at best.

Bella began working and took to it like a pro. It did not take long before she was quickly sought after for various modeling positions. Her reputation of being easy to work with, always on time and constantly a professional brought her vast exposure to all the important fashion houses. They all had their fill of the Prima Donna models and Bella was a refreshing change. They all wanted her to work with them.

She eventually picked several houses to do her modeling for and began traveling to Paris, London, and Barcelona for several shows a year representing these fashion houses. She was in high demand and she loved every moment.

Before her 21st birthday, she was featured on the cover of several fashion magazines and she became quite a celebrity. All the talk show hosts wanted to have her on for an interview and she handled it all so well that many believed she had been doing it for years. The truth is she had been practicing this since she was a little girl and it was a dream come true for her.

That first year of sharing an apartment with Sophia had proved to be quite an ordeal for Bella. She saved up her money and was able to obtain an apartment in an area of the fashion district that was considered almost unattainable. A client of hers knew someone who knew someone who was able to get their hands on an efficiency apartment on the 3rd floor of a brownstone walkup located about 4 blocks from her home base fashion house. Bella cried with joy when she found out she was accepted and could move in that coming weekend.

Bella was so excited she called Sophia immediately upon getting the good news. She wanted to give Sophia the news that she would be moving out. Sophia was not at all happy as who was going to pay the portion of rent and utilities that Bella was paying. This was not a good thing for Sophia and she made sure that Bella knew how unhappy she was. Their relationship had been strained recently when Bella won several modeling jobs that Sophia had requested. Due to the strain those issues caused Bella thought that Sophia would be happy that she was moving out. Apparently not. And, after living with Sophia that year she had learned how vindictive Sophia could be. Now Bella was in a dilemma as to how to handle this quietly without too much of a fuss.

Bella went to the only person that could help her. That was Evie. Evie could see into the near future as to what would happen and it had proven to be 100% accurate if you took her advice.

After speaking with Evie and explaining the situation, Evie told her not to worry and to let her take care of it. When Evie hung up with Bella, Evie immediately called Eleanor and a gathering was set up for that evening.

Two days later, Bella was at the Fashion House when Sophia came up to her all excited. Bella asked her what she was excited about.

"I have been called back to Paris for a long contract (over a year) and I must leave at once. Seems our living arrangement has solved itself. I wish you luck Bella and maybe we will see one another when you are over in Paris for one of the shows. Ciao" … was the last word Bella heard as Sophia had turned her back and was walking away. Bella smiled a knowling smile.

With the Sophia issue handled Bella went back to the apartment and started putting all her personal items into boxes and organized herself for the move. She also needed to purchase some furniture for the new place so she visited several furniture stores and made her selections. She also visited a little shop just down the street from her new apartment that had kitchen items that she would need so she purchased what she thought would provide her the basics needed to set up her kitchen. Later she would laugh as she never cooked a meal in that apartment the entire time she lived there.

The move went smoothly as there were not many things to move out of the apartment shared with Sophia. Mostly her personal items. She moved in Saturday morning and her furniture arrived that afternoon. She was quite pleased with herself as to her selections and the little efficiency apartment was now looking very warm and inviting. Perfect for her. AND, she was never going to have another roommate. The Sophia experience cured her of that situation. Besides, she really missed having her personal space and now when she put something down it would stay where she put it until she wanted it again. This pleased Bella greatly.

Life in the fashion industry assumed its crazy schedule. Bella worked all hours of the day and was always pleased to be able to go to her own private place to relax when work was done. Her popularity continued to climb and if she went out on the town with her friends it was crazy with paparazzi. They would have to find ways to sneak into clubs or restaurants via the back door to avoid the crowds following her.

The Sisterhood of Hamp's Bayou came to visit her often and were amazed at her popularity and they all loved it just the same. It was so much fun hanging out with such a famous person.

CHAPTER 2

European Adventure

Bella was becoming quite the celebrity in the fashion industry. She was being featured on every industry magazine and had several offers from the top fashion houses to work with them exclusively. Her agent was constantly presenting opportunities for her to go to Europe and do various shows. After turning several of those proposals down she finally agreed to accept one to try out the experience. She had never thought of working outside of the United States but her agent said this was the next step for her. So she applied for her first passport and began packing for her trip to Paris. She was barely in her mid-20's and she was in high demand. Life simply did not get any better than this.

This trip to Paris proved to be just the thing to get Bella motivated in her industry again. Things were done so differently in Europe and she got excited again about the total experience. She also managed to run into Sophia again and they had a great reunion. Seemed Sophia was glad to have come back to Paris and she took Bella everywhere to be introduced to all the movers and shakers in the industry. Before long, the paparazzi were following them everywhere. A whole new life was being exposed to Bella and she was thriving on it.

Bella and Sophia became inseparable as several houses requested them both for shows coming up. They both accepted and worked as a team. Both were successful and professional models and were both sought after heavily. Bella spent about 14 months in Paris and worked alongside Sophia for many of the shows. They became the talk of the town and were invited to dozens of parties throughout the elite of the city. Everyone wanted them.

Bella's first love disappointment happened in Paris when she met this dazzling young man who swept her off her feet. They met at one of the parties that Sophia managed to drag her to. Peter worked for one of the fashion houses as part of the management team that organized the fashion shows. Bella was so impressed with his professionalism and knowledge. She could listen to Peter for hours as he explained how it all worked from his side of the runway. Even though Bella knew Peter was a player, she fell for him anyway. Bella could not help herself. She was totally taken by his charisma.

Then the inevitable happened. Bella had become accustomed to just entering Peter's apartment whenever she was in the area. She seldom knocked as she was the only person, she knew of that would be in his apartment.

It was a perfect day with the sun shining overhead, all her work completed for the day and her heart racing to be with the man she loved. She raced to Peter's apartment and ran up the stairs to his landing. She opened the door and raced in yelling, "Hi my darling, I am here. Let's have some fun and enjoy this perfect day." While yelling out for Peter she noticed several pieces of female clothing laying around that did not belong to her. She was instantly alerted and moved to the bedroom where the door was slightly ajar. This is not normal so she flung the door open to find Peter and another woman totally naked in his bed.

Bella's entry into the bedroom had totally startled the two people who had been enthralled in their love making and did not hear her come in. Peter quickly wrapped himself in the top sheet and hopped out of bed and ran over to Bella, who was standing there with her mouth wide open in shock.

Peter began with, "Bella, please let me try to explain this. It is not as it appears." ….. as he watched Bella running for the front door.

All Bella could think to say was… "Really?" She looked him straight in his eyes and then simply and quietly turned around to walk out of the apartment. She was too proud to let him think he hurt her. She never looked back as she walked out, slammed his entry door behind her and ran down the stairs while the tears were running down her face.

When the sun hit her face as she hit the street in a fast run out of his building, Bella didn't care who saw her at this time. She was in total disgust as to what she just saw. She was crushed at the disloyalty of Peter. She heard Sophia's words about do not trust that guy as he is a player. "I am warning you," were Sophia's last words to her about Peter. She was right. Oh how Bella hated to have to admit that Sophia was right.

It took Bella several weeks to get over the hurt that Peter caused her. She continued to go to parties with Sophia but avoided any kind of hook up that may have presented itself to her with another man. She wasn't sure she even liked men at this point in her life. And that no-good son-of-a Peter continuing to call her to apologize just made her madder. She would just hang up without saying a word. Eventually he quit calling.

Bella finished her contract work and returned to New York City. She was happy to be back in the States. She could not wait to get back to her own place and just relax for a few weeks. No contracts and no work to worry about for a couple of weeks and she was going to enjoy the relaxation.

When she called her sisters back in Hamp's Bayou she was thrilled to learn they were coming to NYC to visit with her. She began instantly to book hotel rooms right up the street from her little apartment. She booked one for herself as well so that she could stay close to these women who were her most prized people in the world.

Bella purchased tickets to the hottest Broadway play and arranged for a spectacular dinner at one of NYC's finest Italian restaurants. This was going to be incredibly special for her and she wanted these very dear women to have the best time ever.

Bella sent a limo to pick them up at the airport and bring them to the hotel. She was waiting in the lobby when they got there and the reunion was heartwarming. After all the hugs, Bella got them registered for their rooms and got everyone their room keys. She then moved them to the elevator to go up to her suite where she had champaign chilling to celebrate their arrival. Their suitcases were being taken to their individual rooms for them by the Bell Captain and staff. All previously arranged by Bella. They were all next door to one another with connecting doors. Again, all compliments of Bella.

Bella escorted the sisters to her suite and then poured champaign after they ooo'd and aaah'd at the view out of the floor to ceiling windows overlooking Times Square in her living room. Bella's heart was signing as she was so incredibly happy to have these very special women close to her again. She finally felt at peace.

Eleanor said with a giggle." Wow, this champaign is really hitting me hard but I am loving it.

"Bella, this place is amazing and this view is simply unbelievable. I speak for all of us and just want you to know, we are so happy to see you and look forward to spending the next few days with you,' cheered Eleanor.

"Everyone, please lift your glass" … (as Eleanor begins the toast) … "to the Sisterhood. We are back together and ready to have some fun!"

The glasses all clinked together as everyone yelled …" Hear-Hear" … and they all downed the champaign. The giggling started shortly thereafter as they continued to drink the champaign and recall memories of their past times together. Each one seemed to recall a particular memory that meant something to them and the entire group.

After each memory, another toast was made to "The Sisterhood". And, of course more giggling. It was a grand reunion.

After a few hours, Bella said… "As much as I am loving this moment, it is nearly 4:00 pm and I have dinner reservations made for us for 7:00 so you probably need to get yourselves cleaned up from your travels and possibly spilled champaign." Everyone laughed as they knew she was right; so sadly they said goodbye for now and agreed to meet in the lobby at 6:30. Each one headed out the door to their respective room after kissing Bella and giving her a hug. Bella smiled to herself as she looked down the hall at them holding hands and headed for their rooms. It was such a delight to see them again and she was so happy they were here with her.

Eleanor got to her room first. She slid the keycard in the slot to open the door to a magnificent room. It had floor to ceiling windows as well and she just stood for a moment in pure amazement at just how beautiful the room was. It had a living room area and the bedroom was in a separate room. She was duly impressed. She noticed some fresh flowers on a side table with a note. She walked over to the table and pulled the note out of the crisp white envelope. The note was from Bella, welcoming her. Tears welled up in Eleanor's eyes as she loved Bella so much and this was such a beautiful gesture on Bella's part. This is going to be a fabulous trip. Eleanor was sure of it.

Luna and Evie got settled in their rooms and they all agreed to meet in the hallway in 60 minutes, which gave them time to shower and dress for dinner. Eleanor checked with everyone with 10 minutes to spare to make sure all were on target for the hallway meeting. One last peek at herself in the full-length mirror behind the bedroom door. Yes, she was as ready as she was ever going to be and out the door she went.

Eleanor knocked on each one's door as they stepped out into the hallway to head to Bella's room. All were refreshed and ready to enjoy a fun evening together. They all turned and headed down the hallway when Bella's door flew open and she jumped out into the hallway to greet them. They all laughed and ran to hug Bella. It was so wonderful to be together again and the joy permeated the hallway. Hand in hand they strolled together towards the elevator.

Bella had made reservations and arrangements at one of her favorite Italian restaurants a few blocks away but due to paparazzi she secured a limo to drive them. She also arranged that they be escorted in thru the kitchen so not to attract a crowd at the entry. She had learned to prepare in advance as she always seemed to attract a crowd regardless of where she went.

When the elevator doors opened to the lobby, Bella was already aware of eyes watching them as they moved out of the elevator. She quickly ushered her friends forward as fast as she could towards the front door, but several folks jumped in front of them to snap pictures. Eleanor jumped back a little started and so did Luna. Evie was grinning from ear to ear as if she already knew this would happen.

Bella grabbed their arms and moved them outside directly into the limo to save them from the onslaught of camera's being raised for pictures. Once inside Bella exclaimed…" I am so sorry for that to happen. It is something I deal with so much and it is very annoying at times."

They all laughed and had just settled into their seats in the limo when they arrived at the restaurant. The limo pulled up in the alleyway and the driver opened the back door to let them exit. Bella jumped out first and went to the kitchen door of the restaurant. The owner was waiting for her and happily opened the door for all of them to escape out of the limo and get inside the restaurant. They managed to do just that and not be seen. Bella was grinning and her plan worked.

The owner gave Bella a big hug and showed them all through the kitchen area to a special room he had set up for them to have dinner. They would not be disturbed and could enjoy a great evening without people interrupting them for pictures, or autographs, etc. Again, Bella was very pleased that her arrangements had been honored and she would make sure everyone knew how accommodating Anthony was at his restaurant.

As he exited the room promising to return with the wine for the evening, Bella leaned over and whispered into Anthony's ear....

"Thank you, my friend. You have done me a great honor this evening and I will never forget your generosity." Anthony did not respond but smiled, looked Bella in the eyes, nodded and exited the room.

The sisters were impressed. The room was beautifully decorated and candles were lit everywhere. The pale salmon colored tablecloth offered rich elegance without being too much. The china was exquisite and appropriate for the table setting. Everything had a magical feel to it and the sisters all grabbed hands as if they needed to touch one another to confirm they were there together. The sheer comfort in that hand holding seemed to have settled in all their souls at the same time as they looked at one another and simultaneously released their holds and settled into their chairs.

"Wow is all I can say".... said Eleanor as the first to speak.

"Same for me"... said Evie and Luna chiming in at almost the same time. "I love this room. It is so romantic but not over the top. Know what I mean girls?" continued Evie, and they all nodded in agreement.

Bella was thrilled that they were impressed. Anthony entered the room carrying several bottles of wine that he had selected for their evening at the prior request of Bella. Bella winked at Anthony as he approached the table and presented the first bottle to Bella.

Bella nodded and said..."Ladies, this wine comes from Paris and I was introduced to it when I lived there. It is amazing and I hope that you will enjoy it as much as I do."

After the wine was placed in each of their glasses, Bella tapped her glass and asked for a toast.

Bella continued…"I have been looking forward to seeing you my dear sweet sisters for so long. We are finally back together again and my heart is singing. You bring me so much joy and I have missed you dearly. Let's promise to not go so long again between visits with one another. And, let's also agree to just have fun and enjoy each other this visit."

And with that, Bella raised her glass and the sisters followed. They all touched each other's glass, yelled "hear-hear" and drank their wine. And so the evening began.

CHAPTER 3

David

Several months later Bella was booked for a fashion trip to Barcelona. She met a man named David Tomas that she was completely in awe of. He was a Spaniard by nationality and culture. He was opening his financial planning business in Barcelona and just happened to be at the courthouse the same time Bella was. He was tall, dark, and handsome and had a rich, romantic accent when he spoke. What every girl dreams of or at least what Bella was dreaming of.

David happened to be at the courthouse in Barcelona to change the spelling of his last name to Thomas versus the Spanish version of Tomas. He wanted to be more Americanized.

Bella happened to be at the courthouse that very same day doing a photo shoot of the new business attire clothing line of the fashion house she was working for that week. It was kismet as they would tell others in years to follow.

David was leaving the building when he ran right into Bella who was heading inside to visit the restroom. They collided and looked shocked at first and then started to laugh. Bella began apologizing for not paying attention.

David couldn't believe how beautiful this woman was that he was hanging on to and could only stare at her. He couldn't seem to let go of her. And her smile took his breath away. He just kept staring.

He didn't hear her saying…"I am so sorry. I didn't see you. Do you speak any English?" With no answer Bella assumed he didn't speak English and she was calling for a translator to help her.

One of the staffers came rushing to her side and began to translate what she was saying to the man who was holding on to her.

Finally David realized what was happening and said…" Oh… I am so sorry. You just surprised me so much that I was lost for words. I speak English and I too am sorry but only that I haven't run into you until now. Where have you been all my life?"… and then he laughed out loud at how ridiculous that sounded.

Both David and Bella were laughing together and he finally let go of her. She excused herself as she was on a mission and needed to find the ladies room post haste. They both again laughed and she marched off towards the women's bathroom.

David watched her walk away and couldn't believe what he was watching. Her stature was stunning and he was mesmerized. She stood about 5'10" and was perfectly shaped. Her long ebony hair just bounced along with every step. He realized that he had to get to know her better. This could be the woman of his dreams. He had to find out.

He waited outside the women's bathroom for her to exit. When she came out he jumped in front of her and said…" Now that I have run into you again, literally, I need to know more about you. Will you have dinner with me tonight?".

Bella looked at him, smiled and said, "I have plans for this evening but possibly another night? Will that work for you?" She had another photo shoot that night at one of the night clubs in town and would be tied up late. She was intrigued by this man and she also wanted to find out more about him.

"How about tomorrow night" … he quickly added. She smiled and nodded her head in agreement and one of the staff from the photo shoot came over to get her to return to work. As she was walking away, she told him to pick her up at her hotel lobby at 7:30 the next evening and he agreed.

David again watched her walk away being escorted by a couple of handlers from the photo shoot. He watched her work for a few minutes and was impressed by her professionalism and talent.

He then remembered he didn't even know her name. He went up to one of the workers at the photo shoot and asked what her name was.

"Sir, that is Bella. She is a famous American model who is doing work for us here in Barcelona" … was his answer.

This man was also entranced by her beauty and talent. David could totally understand why every man who ever saw her would be entranced as well.

All he could think of was… "WOW. How did I get so lucky to get to have dinner with her"?

David spent the next day planning an incredible evening of fine dining and slow dancing. He wanted to get this woman into his arms and never let her go. He was already crazy for her and they only exchanged a couple of words. How can this happen? Thank goodness Delgado was leaving him alone for a change.

The lobby of Bella's hotel was very busy as it was THE 5-star hotel in Barcelona. Many tourists were milling about and joining others. He picked a spot to watch the elevators for when Bella would come into the lobby. He was as nervous as he was on his very first date with a woman many years ago. This seemed so silly but he wanted to make this a very special night.

David was scanning the room when suddenly, he sees Bella heading towards him. She looked amazing and his jaw dropped open at her beauty. She walked with such grace and the baby pink dress she had on against her dark skin and dark hair seemed to light up the whole room. People all looked in her direction as she drew all the attention to her. She was dressed simply but elegant and he jumped up to go to meet her quickly.

"You look amazing" …was all he could get out. Bella smiled back at him and said, "Why thank you sir".

He took her arm and escorted her outside the hotel to the street where he hailed a taxi to take them to dinner. He did not expect to have the attention that hit them once Bella came out into public on the street. The paparazzi went crazy and cameras were going off everywhere.

David quickly ushered Bella into a cab and they sped away from the crowd. Bella said," Thank you for getting me out of there so quickly. I am not sure why my presence causes that kind of reaction" and David knew why and just smiled.

"I promise we won't have this happen during dinner, said David as he grabbed his cellphone and made a phone call.

Bella didn't understand Spanish enough to know what he was saying but she knew it had to do with where they were going for dinner. And she was happy to know that he wasn't looking for the limelight and wanting to just hang out with someone who was a celebrity. She had been on many of those type of dates and they were no fun at all. This was indeed a refreshing change which made her smile.

The taxi pulled down an alleyway and stopped. David stepped out and told her to wait for a moment. When he returned, he grabbed her hand and helped her out of the taxi after he checked to make sure the area was clear of anyone.

He escorted Bella in through the back door of a restaurant. The Maître D had been notified that they were there and greeted David with a handshake and smile and motioned for them to follow him.

David and Bella followed the Maître D to a small room with only 1 pre-set table and several side tables and pulled out a chair for Bella. She thanked him and sat down. David sat down across the table from her. She was smiling at him as he had such a large smile on his face, she couldn't help but smile back.

A server appeared quickly and offered to pour some wine. David asked Bella if she wanted some and she nodded. David sampled the wine and nodded to pour Bella some of this beautifully light chardonnay wine selected by the Maître D for them.

The room was dimly lit and the only light was coming from the candles lit on the table and at other side tables in the room. It gave off such a beautiful aura into the room and was very romantic in Bella's eyes. There was soft music playing in the background and it made you feel as if you were out in the country away from all the noise and craziness of a big city.

They exchanged some idle chat for a few minutes when David asked Bella… "Would you do me the honor of dancing with me? This song playing now just happens to be one of my favorites."

Bella agreed and stood up and he took her hand and walked her over to another area away from the table and pulled her into his arms. They seemed to fit together rather nicely.

Bella started to pull back a little but changed her mind as it felt wonderful to be in his arms. He seemed to make her feel so safe and secure. It felt so different for her as she has been on the go for so many years and always being in the limelight never gave her any feeling like this. She was enjoying this moment while it lasted.

David had taken the liberty of ordering their dinner and Bella enjoyed all the flavors of the dishes he had selected. She was amazed at his uncanny ability to know what she liked. Of course, she had no idea that he had contacted her agent to find out what she liked so he could surprise her and it worked. She was genuinely pleased with his efforts.

After they had eaten and shared stories with one another about their families and growing up, Bella was totally enamored with David and his personality seemed to just blend with hers. They laughed at some of the silly antics they shared with one another and Bella introduced David intuitively to her sisterhood of friends that were as much a part of her life as her brothers and parents were.

Soon the evening would come to a close as Bella had an early rise morning photo shoot that had to have her up and ready by 4 am. David agreed to get her back to the hotel early enough for her to get her beauty rest, so to speak and he agreed as long as she agreed to see him again the next evening.

Bella said… "I would love to see you again tomorrow night and we won't have to end so early as I don't have any shoot time scheduled the following day. Believe it or not, I am clear for that day".

And with that information David's brain started to formulate plans for the next time they are together. He asked her when she would be free and she stated her photo shoot would be over by 11:00 am and she was clear after that thru the next day.

The taxi arrived at her hotel to drop her off and David escorted her to the lobby elevator. She did not ask him to come up to her room and he did not attempt to make that kind of move on her. He simply bent down and gave her a gentle kiss on her lips as the door opened to the elevator.

He whispered…. "Until tomorrow. Good night, Bella".

She stepped into the elevator and said … "Good Night David… I will see you tomorrow" … and the doors closed.

Both of them were grinning ear to ear looking at the closed elevator doors. David finally pried himself away and went back to his apartment a few blocks away.

Bella was almost in a trance like state when she got back to her room. All she could think about was calling the sisters and telling them about this incredible man that she met. She would have to wait as she needed to get some sleep. BUT she was going to have to tell them all about this meeting and how it happened. Her dream had finally come true after so many previous disasters.

It didn't take David long to get his plan for their next meeting. He would make it a memorable event. He would plan a picnic lunch and take her for a drive out into the country and away from the maddening crowds and the paparazzi. She needed her break from all that and he wanted her undivided attention.

He called her after 11 the next day as he knew she would be finished with her photo shoot. He connected with her on the first try.

"Hey there pretty lady. Are you free this afternoon to take a little ride out to the country," he asked when she answered the phone?

"Why yes I am free this afternoon and that sounds delightful. I would love to go for a ride and see some of Spain that I can't see here in the city. What time shall I expect you to pick me up?" she asked politely.

"Well, I was thinking that we could take that ride and possibly find a quaint little place to stay overnight and come back tomorrow evening sometime. How does that sound to you?" he asked while holding his breath for her answer.

"I think that would be great fun and a perfect way for me to relax and enjoy the surroundings and the company. I will be ready by 1 if that isn't to late. I will need to pack an overnight bag, etc." she said with her heart beating a hundred times a minute.

David just about jumped for joy and tried everything to make sure he didn't sound too excited… "that sounds perfecto. I will pick you up at 1:00. I will meet you in your hotel lobby. See you at 1:00 pretty lady."

And they both hung up and they both had broad grins again on their faces. This was just way too exciting.

Bella instantly picked up her phone to call Eleanor and she needed to tell her all about David. She got Eleanor on the first try and said…" Hey there sister, I just had to call you and see how you are doing and fill you in on what is happening here. Do you have a minute to chat?"

"I always have time for you Bella dear" … said Eleanor. She had just started to eat dinner but put her fork down. Bella never just calls out of the blue so Eleanor needed to find out what was happening.

Eleanor questioned…" So tell me sweetie, what is happening in Barcelona that would make you call me during dinner hour?" Laughing as she said the words and wondering internally if this was going to be good or bad news.

Bella was giggling like a school girl and said… "Well dear Eleanor, I hope I didn't interrupt your dinner BUT, I have found my man. You remember my dream from when I was little about finding my Prince Charming by running into him… well that exact thing happened and I have met the most incredible man. I know that there is nobody as grand as your Blaine but this man is going to be a close second. HAHAHA". And Bella just burst out laughing and couldn't help being so giddy.

Bella went on to tell the story of how they met and that first date and how romantic it was and that they were heading out this afternoon for a ride in the country and an overnight somewhere together. Eleanor couldn't get a word in as Bella just kept gushing on and on about how she was crazy already about this man. Eleanor was smiling just listening to Bella carrying on. She had never seen her like this with the exception of getting that first modeling job back when she was 19. Wow, that was a long time ago.

"Bella darlin. You sound so happy. My only advise dear sweet sister is to take your time and make sure he is really the right man for you. I know you have had some tough times with some of the men you have met but remember those lessons and take it slow. OKAY?" said Eleanor trying to make sure Bella understands and doesn't get hurt again.

Bella has had her fair share of hurt over the years and all any of the sisters wanted was to take care of each other and not see anyone hurt. She loved them for their concern.

Bella answered," But of course. I have to many scars on my heart to let another one happen again so yes, I am taking it slow. I am just so happy now and believe this man is different. My David is caring, considerate and thoughtful. I just don't think he would do anything that would hurt me. BUT, for you and all my sisters, I promise to take it easy and slow with this one. Okay?".

Eleanor smiled and Bella blew kisses through the phone and they hung up. Bella was still bouncing around and putting some items into an overnight pack.

Eleanor had a worried look on her face. She would call the other sisters and bring them up to speed on this conversation. Evie will be needed to check the near future with this one in Bella's life.

Bella is packed and ready and practically runs to the elevator to meet David in the lobby. She is running a little behind as she called her agent to let her know she would be out of town overnight and that she would call her once she knows where she will be staying. That conversation didn't go well as her agent was worried about her running off with a man, she just met in a country she didn't know how to speak the language to get help if she needed it. These were all excellent points and Bella knew that her agent was right, but it didn't stop her from going anyway.

David was in the lobby pacing as it was after 1:00 and Bella is not one to be late. He was dreading the fact that maybe she changed her mind and wasn't coming after all. Maybe it was too much to assume as it was only their second date and was he moving too fast? Something inside him said he wasn't yet; she is late and maybe she had changed her mind. Fear and regret were starting to set in when he sees her almost running towards him.

"I am so sorry for being a bit late. I was on the phone with my agent and she kept talking and I couldn't get her off the phone." She was practically yelling this as she raced towards him.

He grabbed her and put his finger over her mouth to quiet her. He then gave her a long kiss and just held her for a moment. She collapsed in his arms and instantly felt relieved and at peace. This was exactly what she needed, and she was falling for this incredible man that she just assured Eleanor that she would take it slow with him. Right now, all of that is flying out the window as this just felt too incredible to let go.

David grabbed her overnight bag and her arm and they both were laughing as they exited the lobby. David's car was sitting out front and he threw her overnight bag into the trunk of his car. It was a convertible and he opened the side door and helped Bella inside.

He yelled… "Buckle up" as he went around to the other side of the car to get in.

Bella looked up at the brilliant blue sky with no clouds as she buckled her seat belt. She was smiling when she said…"Okay mister, I am buckled up and ready to go on this great adventure you have planned. Is there anything in advance that I should prepare myself for?"

Laughing, David leaned over and said," You my pretty lady are about to have the greatest day of your life. Just sit back and enjoy the ride and the fresh air. The scenery has been especially picked out for your pleasure and enjoyment. Each moment is being given to you as a present in appreciation for your presence."

Bella blushed at that cheesy statement and just smiled and enjoyed the air blowing through her hair as she felt the warm sun hitting her arms and legs. It was March and yet this felt like a new spring day. She reached inside her handbag and pulled out a headband to pull her hair back to keep it from flying all over the place. She wanted to watch and see every moment of the countryside they were driving through.

The ride was spectacular. They drove for about an hour and went through olive fields and grape vineyards. They stopped at a little roadside area to share in a bottle of wine and a light snack that David had prepared.

His little roadside picnic was delightful and gave them some time to be close and talk. He explained about some of the vineyards they had passed and that he knew some of the owners and loved their wines. They were drinking one of the Chardonnay's from one of the vineyards they had driven through. It was light and refreshing. Bella was impressed with his knowledge of wines and the countryside.

They got back in the car and continued the drive down the coast to a city named Valencia. She had never been there and David began to tell her about the carnival. They celebrate St. Joseph's Day there and he was taking her to experience that event.

They pulled up to the hotel where he had made advance arrangements and she got out of the car and walked over to admire the view from the steps leading down to the road and the beach below. The view of the Mediterranean from that spot was spectacular and she took out her camera to take a picture. She wanted to remember that view.

David gave her a little hug and said he would be right back. He went inside to check them in and get the key to their room. He spoke with the desk clerk briefly and then came out to join Bella who was still standing in the same spot. She could not move as the beauty of that view kept her mesmerized.

"This is just so beautiful David. I had to take a picture so I could remember it. Thank you for bringing me here." said Bella as he came up beside her and wrapped his arm around her shoulder and pull her closer to him.

"Wait until you see the sunset. It will take your breath away." He said as he indicated they had more to see and moved her to step down and walk down the steps.

As they walked down the steps there were flowers blooming everywhere. Spring had sprung here and it was unbelievable how beautiful everything was. All the structures were painted a brilliant white and the flowers were all red and orange and the deep greens associated with their foliage. It was difficult to soak it all in and Bella was totally in awe of the majesty of the colors.

"Bella, please come over here and sit with me so we can watch the parade" … said David who had left her standing and staring at all the blooms.

She moved over to where he was and sat next to him and he moved slightly to bring up a bottle of red wine and two glasses that just hapened to be placed there for him (as he requested with the front desk person).

He poured them each a glass of wine and then Bella saw that just below them was a winding street going through the city and there was a parade with a fiesta kind of atmosphere all around. They had perfect seats to watch as floats, walkers and bands paraded by. Everyone was having a fabulous time. Bella was enjoying watching all the revelers and the Pinot Noirwine was especially flavorful and hitting the spot. Bella thought that life couldn't get any better than this.

When the parade was over it seemed that their bottle of wine was exhausted as well. So, they moved up to go to their room and freshen up for dinner. Bella realized that the bellman had taken their overnight bags to their room and had unpacked everything for them and clothes had been laid out for the evening based on what was in their bags.

When they opened their room and found clothes laying out for them, they looked at each other and laughed. Nobody had done that for them since they were kids and Bella only when doing a photo shoot did they lay out what she was to wear. It just caught their funny bones and they giggled together and looked at one another and then they were kissing like they would never see one another again. Maybe it was the wine. Bella wasn't sure. But she was crazy for this man and wanted to be with him.

Bella didn't care at that moment if they ever went to dinner and David was in his own world and was lost in everything about Bella. Soon they were removing the clothes placed so neatly on the bed and pulled the bed spread back. They slowly looked at one another and began to undress each other.

Bella unbuttoned David's shirt and slid her hands down his arms to remove the shirt and then around to his back to hold on to him for a moment. His chest was full of hair and was dark all over. He had been in the sun and had quite a tan. His body was hard and toned and he definitely worked out.

David loosened Bella's hold on him and he moved her away from him as he moved to remove her blouse. He kissed her slowly and deeply. He gently unbuttoned her blouse and slowly slipped it off her. He then kissed her neck and moved her hair to her back. He then lifted her up and carried her to the bed and sat her down on the edge of the bed.

He then knelt down in front of her and removed the rest of her clothing. He slowly began to kiss her neck and felt her respond to his touches. Such gentleness was something Bella had never experienced and she was shocked at how much her body reacted to David's touch.

Bella rocked back and forth with ecstasy as David arose from the kneeling position he was in and lifted her up with him. He continued to kiss her and wake up every nerve in her body. She pulled back from David and took his hand and moved them both to the bed.

They were now both naked and curled up in one another's arms. David pulled Bella closer to him and he kissed her with a deep longing that Bella could feel all the way down to her toes. She looked at David and said …" David, please make love with me" and with that David entered Bella.

He continued to move in rhythm with Bella and kept going as Bella began to experience an orgasm and then another one. Finally, David was ready, and he screamed with an explosive orgasm that had Bella holding on to him for quite a while.

Exhausted, they both laid quietly next to one another unable to speak and trying to recover. Finally David rolled over on his side and kissed Bella gently on her lips and then on her cheeks and then on her eyes. He then propped his head on his hand and looked her intently in the eyes and said…" You my darling are an amazing lover and you brought me such pleasure. Thank you." And he kissed her again ever so gently.

Bella had tears in her eyes and looked at him and said," You dear sweet David have shown me what can really be experienced when someone wants to love you like you are important to them. Thank you for making me feel like that". And with that said, Bella moved up and leaned into him and kissed him with such passion that it took his breath away.

They laid together for a little while until they realized that it was getting dark outside and that they should get up and get a bite to eat. Bella ran to jump in the shower first laughing all the way and David soon joined her. They proceeded to shower together and enjoyed the intimacy of that moment. They had a hard time keeping their hands off each other from that moment on.

They dressed and went out into the streets of Valencia to enjoy the fiesta and the bonfires all over the city. They found a quaint little restaurant down one of the alley streets that only had about 8 tables in it and nobody was there. They felt like this was meant to be so they ran inside and sat down right away and the owner of the establishment came out to see what they wanted. He said he was closed but would fix them something to eat as he was happy to have a couple so in love it was obvious in his restaurant. With that said… they both laughed so hard it brought tears to their eyes.

During dinner they talked about how Bella missed the sunset as she was busy doing something else far more important and then Bella said, "We will have to come back again soon so I can see that sunset".

David said, "I will bring you here anytime you want to come. This is now our place and we will always remember this day."

And so, the relationship went on to become something that neither one had expected. The love between them was so strong and deep and brought them both joy.

They were together every day and when it came time for Bella to return to NYC, David announced that he was moving to NYC as well as he could not be without his Bella. He could run his financial planning business in NYC just as well as he could in Barcelona. He would just have different clientele. He had not told Mr. Delgado this yet and was not sure how he would take that.

So, the rest of their story is as you would figure it. They moved back to NYC and found a larger apartment to share together. They made plans to get married and the Sisterhood of Hamp's Bayou took charge of planning the event. This would be the 2nd marriage of the group and Eleanor and Blaine had set the precedence of all future sister weddings.

Life continued to be blissful for this couple as David's business was taking off thanks to Bella's influence with various people who she suggested they see David to plan their financial futures.

Bella continued modeling and David would escort her whenever she had to go to Paris or London or even back to Barcelona.

While the sisterhood was planning the wedding, David planned to take Bella back to Valencia for a little get away as she had been working so hard and she needed to see that sunset that they missed that first time they were there. He surprised her at dinner one night and said,

"Sweetheart, I have a surprise for you. Please pack your suitcase and have your passport as we are going back to Valencia to watch that sunset you missed."

And Bella had tears well up in her eyes as she had been thinking about how she could use a trip like that just now as she was exhausted. She got up from her chair and went around to kiss her future husband and thank him for thinking of her as he had.

They arrived in Madrid and then decided to drive across Spain to Valencia as another part of their adventure so Bella could see more of this beautiful country. They arrived in Valencia and David had made all the arrangements just as he had before. This time it was not St. Joseph Day and there was no celebration going on however, the wine was again placed next to the bench they would sit on to watch the sunset. David poured Bella her glass of wine and he asked her if she would be willing to marry him right then and there.

She looked at him and said… "David, I will marry you any time, any place and anywhere you would like." And then she leaned in to kiss him.

David then stood up and motioned to someone who came out from around the corner and he was carrying a book. In this book was a marriage license and he was able to marry them right there on that spot. No fanfare, no big party afterwards and only two witnesses who happened to be maids at the hotel they were staying in. David had set all this up in advance as well hoping that Bella would be agreeable. If not, she would never know he had all this planned in advance.

After the I Do's were said and David put a stunning 3 karat diamond ring on her hand, they were officially married according to the laws of Spain. The magnificent sunset she had been waiting to see was happening right before her eyes and Bella was the happiest she had ever been. She was totally in love with David and willing to spend the rest of her life with him by her side. Life was perfect in her world.

After the brief ceremony David ushered Bella to the same little restaurant they had visited that first time they were there for St. Joseph's Day celebration. The owner was still the same and David had contacted him in advance as well and he prepared a wonderful dinner for the two of them. They had the restaurant to themselves, and that didn't happen very often in their lives. Bella's celebrity status always caused a commotion everywhere they went so this was a unique change for them that they thoroughly enjoyed.

The rest of their stay in Spain was delightful and David had done an exceptional job in planning many excursions and day trips around the area with even a full day at the beach which also never happens often. Bella thought she was beyond happy and hoped that nothing would ever change this feeling she has inside for this incredible man that she loved with all of her being.

Then it hit her she would need to call her sisters and advise that the wedding they were planning would no longer be necessary.

The next day David was going to be gone all day on business so Bella called Eleanor to tell her of the surprise that David had arranged and that they were now husband and wife and hopefully the sisters will understand.

Eleanor screamed for joy and said ….” But of course we will all understand. It is your happiness that we want and have always wanted. Wait until I tell the girls what has happened. Everyone will be so happy. Now you must let us throw you a celebration party here in the Bayou. Not in NYC. This is your home and we want you all to ourselves. Promise?” … Eleanor asked to a smiling Bella on the other end of the phone.

“You know I could never deny you that Eleanor. I know you all have worked so hard on the preparations and now we can just have a party. I will call you when we get back stateside. Okay?” … and Bella hung up the phone beaming with a huge smile as her life couldn’t get any better than it was right at that very moment.

Bella then called her parents to break the news to them. Her mother cried over the phone as she was sorry she wasn’t there to witness her beautiful daughter get married but she understood. After a few minutes of happy cries and congratulations given by her parents to David as well, they hung up agreeing to talk again when they get back to NYC.

They spent a few more days exploring the area and then headed back to Madrid for their return flight home. Bella was so happy with her life and David also seemed happy but there was something bothering him, Bella couldn't figure it out. She kept asking him but he said it was only some business issues and had nothing to do with their relationship.

Bella later found out that he had lost a client that had a rather large sum of money invested with him and it was causing him some stress. Bella found another investor for him and he became his old self again.

Life was returning to normal. Funny how it was the simple things that got rid of stress and worry. This was easy for Bella to help fix and she didn't want David to know it came from her.

And David did not want Bella to know anything about Mr. Delgado. David had a long conversation with him while they were in Valencia on their honeymoon. Things were going to be a little different going forward.

They found a lovely home they decided to purchase on Long Island and they would commute to NYC every day. They had a driver that would pick them up every morning and drive them into the city. They didn't have to worry too much about the commute as they weren't driving and they got a lot of work done in the back seat of the car while riding. Bella would be dropped off first at her office and then David would go on to his office which was only a couple of blocks away. This routine worked out rather well for them both for the next few years.

On a trip back to Hamp's Bayou they decided to purchase a home there and Bella found the exact house she wanted with Evie's help. How did Evie know so much about all the homes that were there? You just had to tell her what you wanted and she found it and it had just about everything you ever wanted or what was on your wish list. If it wasn't part of the property, she would make it happen for you by the time you closed on the property.

This made life so much easier for Bella as now she could come back to the Bayou and see her family and sisters. David began to see just how important the sisters were to Bella over the years and he respected their friendship. There would always be an understanding for David that these women meant the world to Bella and there was no changing that.

Over the years, David would see that Bella would get an invitation in the mail to attend some event in Hamp's Bayou and regardless of what they had planned she was going to the Bayou. There was never any question about that. He never understood why but finally accepted it for what it was. He could say or do nothing that would ever change her mind. She would always just say it was a requirement that she attend and there was never to be a change to that rule. And there was another thing that he knew. He would "never" want to make any of those women she called sisters mad at him. That scared him a little and he wasn't sure why.

One of the special trips was a couple of years ago when Bella got the telephone call that her mother had a heart attack and that Bella needed to get home asap. The plane couldn't fly fast enough, and Bella just made it to the hospital to speak with her mother for a couple of minutes before she passed away. This broke Bella's heart to lose her mother and her father and brothers were all in deep grief for a while. It took Bella quite some time to overcome this grief. David was very comforting and surprisingly so was Blaine, Eleanor's husband. He genuinely seemed concern for her and for her family. It was curious to Bella but not for long as Blaine was killed in a freak accident several months later.

She was worried about her father, but in the months to follow he found a woman he had worked with at the factory many years before and she was becoming more and more important in her father's life. Bella wasn't sure how she felt about that but decided it was good that her father had someone in his life since her mother was gone. This woman would never replace her mother but she thought she might be able to accept her eventually. And this woman happened to be her assistant Anne's mother. Anne had proven to be an excellent assistant to Bella. She and her mother blended in with the family perfectly.

Bella's brothers both had been married and had their own children now and were doing very well. One had a son and a daughter that were both adorable children. Bella loved them dearly.

Her other brother was doing very well and worked at the same factory that her father retired from. He and his wife only had the one daughter and were hoping to possibly adopt a little girl in the future as they were not able to have any additional children. Bella is going to try to help them out if this becomes a real possibility.

Bella loved her family very much but her sisters were her lifeblood. They always supported her in all her endeavors and her magazine "Bella-Dona" Fashion Magazine was very successful because of their support and encouragement. Her modeling career had made her lots of money that she has wisely invested and helped her beloved husband David get his business off the ground. He is doing so well with his business that Bella felt totally comfortable with their financial position. She was finally the happiest she has ever been and could never imagine what is about to unfold in her life.

CHAPTER 4

David and Anne

Anne's Story

Anne made it her mission to be the best assistant Bella could ever possibly find anywhere. She was determined to get close and be the right hand to Bella at all costs. The additional benefit was that her boss had a husband that was so handsome all the women in town would stop and stare whenever he would appear.

Anne was thrilled to have David pouring his heart out to her as she found it very pleasurable to comfort him. This was almost too easy for her as she knew that looking a lot like Bella was working in her favor. And she would use it however she had to. She began her seduction with simple little smiles at first and then moved on to the more alluring methods she had learned over the years.

Growing up without a father left Anne with an anger inside of her that could not be subdued. It seemed to fester inside of her and grew stronger as she got older.

She had pretty much badgered her mother into admitting who her father was. Anne was 25 years old when she finally got her mother to confess who the man was that fathered her but did not want to be a father to her. She had been trying for many years to get her mother to confess but she always held out saying it would not help her to know who her father was.

Anne wasn't sure why her mother finally confessed. Maybe it was because the wife of her father just recently died, and her mother was feeling a little bit better about confessing. Apparently, the woman who was married to her father didn't know about his infidelity and Anne's mother wanted to keep it quiet. Now that she was dead, the truth could come out.

Anne's mother swore her to secrecy after she told her who her father was. He was still grieving at the loss of his wife and Anne's mother was offering him condolences and was hoping to rekindle their relationship.

Anne's was livid with this idea and told her mother that she would disown her if she ever got back involved with this man again. The rage inside Anne at this time was blowing up and her mother knew that she would need to stay away from this man if she was to ever keep her daughter in her life or confess what her true motive was. She confessed and Anne was no longer angry with her.

Anne was on a mission to learn as much as about this man Charlie, who is her father. She found out about his other children who were her 2 half brothers and sister. The brothers were still in town and had their own families. She could not see getting involved with them in any way as they led different lives from her. However, the girl, her stepsister Bella was in fashion, and had just bought a house locally and was preparing to move back and Anne thought this would be the perfect opportunity to get in close to Bella, the light of her father's eye and Anne's target to get even with her father.

When Anne met Bella face to face in the job interview as Bella's assistant, Anne thought how beautiful Bella was and that she was more determined to bring her down to her knees. This woman grew up with a loving family and a father always there to support her and she had the world by the tail while Anne had nothing. Yes, indeed, this was going to be quite an undertaking that Anne was really looking forward to.

Anne went out of her way to be the perfect Assistant. She learned how to interpret Bella's needs and to always be one step ahead of those needs. She became exceptional in her ability to be the best assistant possible to Bella. There was no doubt that Bella liked her as she was always giving her compliments and how much she appreciated all her work. This made Anne happy as she knew she was becoming well entrenched in Bella's life.

Then of course, there was the icing on the cake, Bella's husband David. She saw him for the first time when he came by to take Bella to lunch one day. Anne nearly fell out of her chair as he was so handsome and charming. She remembered thinking about how much fun she was going to have with him as she lured him away from Bella. She was going to take this very slow and develop it properly.

So then the chase began and Anne managed to work on David very slowly over the next couple of months until he was totally enslaved with her charms. She knew when Bella was away from the office that David would intentionally stop by so he could be alone with her and she always dressed alluringly to tease him as much as possible. This was most definitely working, and David was beside himself with desire for her and she knew it.

David invited her to dinner one evening when Bella was away at a conference. Anne dressed appropriately sexy and drove David crazy all through dinner.

Anne told David the story about a man who was her sperm donor and that he would not be bothered to be a father to her and, that the man still lived in town. After some pressure Anne reluctantly told David who the man was, and David was shocked that it was his Bella's own father. Now he understood why Anne and Bella looked so much alike. Anne swore him to secrecy and he agreed to keep her secret as he thought to himself how he was going to use this information to better himself.

Anne was beside herself on her way over to visit with her mother. She had just had lunch with David and he had told her about moving a great deal of money to Nassau in the Bahamas. Her brain was spinning with all kinds of planning ideas and she needed to run some ideas past her mother first before she did anything else.

She had been really angry with her mother when she began another relationship with Charlie, her father and Bella's father. But after her mother explained why she settled down.

The plan was for Anne's mother to rekindle that relationship and get Bella's father to fall in love with her and then she would take everything he had away from him. She would turn his children against him and give Anne what she has always wanted – revenge on the man who would not be a father to her.

So the two of them schemed and plotted and planned their moves over the next couple of months. Anne couldn't wait to tell her mother about the latest developments with David moving 20 million dollars to the Bahama's and that she had a plan to get that money for the two of them.

Anne pulled up to the small little cottage that was the home she grew up in. Nothing special but it was home. She was happy how her mother kept the place neat and clean. The windows had cute little shutters with flower boxes along the bottom sills. There were always flowers blooming in those boxes. Anne never knew how her mother kept those flowers blooming but she did.

The front porch had two rocking chairs that was a special place to Anne as she and her mother would sit there together and rock away planning the rest of their lives together. Anne pulled up in the stone driveway and headed to the back door as that was the entry to the kitchen and the front door was for company only.

Her mother was at the kitchen table having a cup of coffee when Anne burst through the kitchen door. She hugged her mother and plopped down in a chair across the table from her. "You aren't going to believe what has happened now Mom," said Anne gushing with the news.

Her mother looked up and smiled and said, "Well share away. I need some good news today." With that Anne realized her mother seemed upset and she asked her, "What is going on Mom? Are you okay?"

"I am fine. Just trying to digest some things and having one of those days' sweetie but please… please share your news", her mother exclaimed trying to smile through the whole sentence. She didn't want Anne to know she had met with David and it didn't go well. He was not the pushover Anne thought he was. She could not tell Anne about this.

"Okay. Seems that David has moved 20 million dollars into a separate bank account in Nassau, Bahama's Mom and I am going to be on that account within the next 30 days. Count on it", exclaimed Anne.

"He told me about this account today at lunch and I asked him to not tell Bella until after the show. That will buy me enough time to get my name on that account and set us up for life from there. What do ya think?" Anne was almost out of breath after spewing all that out in one breath.

Her mother just looked at her in total disbelief. Thinking that yes, they could manage to live on 20 million dollars somehow. Hahaha just burst up in her brain all at once like… are you kidding. How fabulous that would be. They would go to some small town somewhere in Europe and get lost among the people and live a comfortable life. She could get into that idea quickly. She knew her daughter would fall in love with someone and go off on her own someday, but she would be sitting pretty for the rest of her life financially and that was something she had always dreamed of herself.

Anne saw her mother kind of drift off to some other place and smiled to herself knowing that her mother was daydreaming. She liked when her mother did that as it gave her motivation to help make her mother's dreams come true as well as her own. Her mother had sacrificed her entire life to provide for her the best that she could, and it was time she made her mother's life as comfortable as possible.

The two of them moved out to the front porch and began their rocking regime and started planning and dreaming of where to live and how their future life would be. These were sweet moments together for these two women as they planned their new lives.

David's Story

David is 40 years old and he is burned out on his business. All these rich people are so demanding, and they want all his time. He is over it. He is also married to a woman who is perpetually working. She loves her business of fashion designing and she is very good at it but there needs to be more play time. Why didn't he see this when he met her and decided to marry her?

Yes, he and Bella had this whirlwind romance that knocked them both off their feet, but once reality set back in the true facts that a whirlwind romance doesn't really start a relationship very well. He had married a woman that was totally committed to her career and her work. She had little to no time for anything else. And, he had tried for years to find get away weekends where they could rekindle their romance, but Bella was always busy with an upcoming show or something. She tried to be kind and romantic, but those efforts were few and far apart. Too far apart for him. He missed their intimacy.

He stopped by Bella's office one day and met her secretary, Anne. He couldn't believe his eyes. She was stunningly beautiful, and he just couldn't take his eyes off her. Her charm had captivated him. She was somewhat embarrassed by his obvious attention and did her best to avoid his eyes. She looked almost identical to his wife which was unbelievable to him.

Over the next few months, he would find ways to stop by Bella's office to either take Bella to lunch or bring her some coffee as he was in the neighborhood. His ultimate goal was to see Anne and to try to get closer to her.

He finally broke her down and got her comfortable with his attention the whole time professing his love of her boss. Anne was beginning to feel a little bit jealous and she knew she had no right to feel that way. This man was married to her boss who has been extra nice to her and besides, she loved her job and didn't want to lose it. Well, this was what she told everyone who would listen to her anyway.

In the last few months David seemed to know when Bella would be out of the office and would stop by pretending to not know that Bella was gone out of town. He professed that he hardly sees Bella anymore and that she works all the time and they never talk or do anything together anymore. He is a lost soul and doesn't know what to do. Did Anne happen to have any advice for him?

And so the new relationship began.

David was still going back and forth to New York City where his financial planning business was still centered. Bella had moved her business back to Hamp's Bayou and he was in the process of moving his to HB as well but until he got all of that arranged, he still had to be in New York City at least once a month. These trips took him away for about a week. The break was good for the both of them as usually by the time came for him to return to NYC they both were ready to have a break from one another.

He also was having some issues with Mr. Delgado who was furious that he had left Barcelona and married Bella. Seems that Mr. Delgado expected David to take care of their joint business in Barcelona indefinitely and David wanted out. Mr. Delgado had sent a message that David meet with him and David flew back to NYC with Bella and never met with Mr. Delgado. It was not a good move on David's part and now there are going to be repercussions of his actions.

All issues aside, David was desperate to find a way to spend some time with Anne. He came up with the idea that he could tell Bella he was in NYC and then could meet Anne in New Orleans which would be perfectly fine for her to get off work to go to NOLA for some sort of girl trip and Bella would buy that completely.

David called Anne to meet him to discuss his idea. She smiled and recalled how she had hinted that maybe they could do a trip to NOLA some time together and now he has come up with this brilliant idea. Yes, she was smiling. They met at a little bar just outside of town and sat in a booth to discuss David's plan. He sat across from her holding her hands as he unveiled his plan. Finally he couldn't stand it and moved to the same side of the booth where she was sitting. He had to kiss her and hold her and touch her perfect skin. She smiled up at him and told him she would love to spend a few days with him in NOLA and he went crazy just thinking about some private time with her. Then they realized that they were still in public and they collected themselves. It felt like someone was watching them so David moved back to the other side of the table.

David began making arrangements in NOLA and planning their little escapade just like he had planned his first trips with Bella in Spain when they first met. He was truly excited to be able to plan this excursion with Anne and was doing everything he could to make it a perfect romantic getaway for the two of them.

In the meantime, David began looking at his financial business and really didn't want to move it to Hamp's Bayou as he felt he needed his freedom to get out of Hamp's Bayou at least once a month. He was not bringing in any new business and it was pretty stagnant. If he had to bring it to Hamp's Bayou, then Bella would get involved again and he didn't want that. He was still in control of her money as well which amounted to 30 million dollars that she totally trusted him with. He used her money as leverage with several of his clients as he developed new clients in the past. His business had about 10 million in trust funds and other financial positions but these were other people's funds and not readily accessible for David.

David decided that he would move some of the money he was entrusted with to an account he would open in the Bahama's and set his business up there as operating a business there had great tax relief implications. He could justify that with Bella if she or any of his other clients asked.

It would be a great cover and once the accounts were opened in his name Bella could not attach it in anyway. He felt relief at that thought and on his last trip to NYC he grabbed a flight to Nassau in the Bahama's and opened his account. He was transparent about moving the funds from Hamp's Bayou as he didn't want any issues. Most of the money he could access was in the Hamp's Bayou account(Eleanor's bank) and he would explain it all to Bella when he got home.

He remembered the bank person contacted someone in Hamp's Bayou to verify him and all seemed to go just fine. He had the account and transferred about 20 million dollars and would move more money later that month. This action also protected the money from Mr. Delgado who seemed to think he was due most of it.

When he returned to the Bayou from the trip to NYC he had every intention of telling Bella about opening the new bank account in Nassau as his new place of business but he got side tracked by Anne. Anne met him the day after he returned for lunch and when he shared what he had done with Anne she explained, "Bella has a lot of things going on now and to drop something like this on her would maybe send her off the deep end. She has a new show coming up and is in the throes of getting everything organized. David, I recommend you hold off on telling Bella about this transfer of money until after the show."

And David agreed to just wait as he has been through one of these shows before with Bella and Anne was right. She gets so involved and really didn't need anything else thrown at her while she was in the middle of this event. David was thrilled that he had Anne to help him do the right thing. She has been such an angel for him, and he was so looking forward to some alone time with Anne once they could get away at the same time.

CHAPTER 5

The Gathering

Over the years the sisters took turns calling their gatherings and overseeing the business of their "sisterhood". The business of the meeting usually had to do with one of them needing support from the others on a particular subject. In high school or college this could have been related to a boyfriend or parental problems. As they got older the issues changed considerably but ultimately related to some sort of action to be taken. They would discuss the problem and determine a resolution. Regardless of the issue at hand, all would have to agree to some form of action to assist or aide the wounded sister. The boyfriend would need a talking to or the parents would have to be persuaded to agree to whatever was needed to be agreed to. Collectively they were very persuasive. One recent gathering had been held on behalf of Bella to resolve the Sophia issue. That issue was fairly easy for the group.

The sisterhood became very proficient at achieving their desires. They all knew they could accomplish anything they wanted to individually and having the aide of the other sisters in that journey to achieve their desires just made it all the easier for them. As they grew up and became more mature the meetings took on different aspects of what needed attending to. Their ritual took on a magical atmosphere and the results were sometimes just as magical.

The front doorbell rang and Bella knew her first dinner guest had arrived and she quickly went to the front door and found Eleanor standing there. They hugged and Bella motioned for Eleanor to enter.

They walked to the living room and Bella went to the bar and poured Eleanor a glass of her favorite bourbon.

It sure felt nice to be in her home in the Bayou and having her sisters for a dinner. Well, dinner and a gathering later. It had been what about 6 years ago since they last were all together for a gathering? As Bella recalled, she had called everyone together because of Blaine. That was not a happy time and there was some dread in her heart for tonight's gathering.

Now Eleanor had called tonight's gathering and Bella had volunteered to host the event. They were visiting with easy catch-up news when the front doorbell rang again.

Claudette, Bella's housekeeper opens the front door to let Luna enter and Evie was right behind her. Both women entered the house and handed their wraps to Claudette who took them and hung them up.

"Hi everyone" … says Luna and Evie together as they enter the room smiling.

Eleanor and Bella turn around towards them and they all get up to get in line to give and receive their hug. This had become another one of their rituals for when they meet up with one another. Evie enjoyed going to each and giving them a warm embrace and a kiss on the cheek.

Bella waited to be the last one in line and when she reached Evie, she said…"and what shall I fix you to drink".

"Humm let me see. I believe I will have a glass of red wine. Wait, what is the meat for dinner?" asked Evie

Bella chimed back "we are having Beef Wellington" for dinner. I trust that will meet with your pallet requirements" … she laughed.

"Red wine it is then…" she announced to Bella.

Bella went over to the bar that was set up on the other side of the room and poured Evie a glass of her finest red wine. She knew Evie would like this wine as it was served to her in NYC when the sisters had come to visit.

Bella presents the red wine to Evie who was chatting with Eleanor and saying something about returning phone calls. Bella asks everyone to raise their glass for a toast. They all stand in a circle holding their glasses up high as Bella presents a toast.

"May this gathering fill your stomachs with life's richest rewards and keep your minds clear and sharp for deliberate conversation"

"Hear-Hear" …they all said and then clinked their glasses together and took a sip of their drink. They all remembered that it is bad luck to do a toast and not drink from your glass. Nobody could remember who told them that, but they all know that somebody's mother was the one who educated them on this protocol.

"Let's sit for a few minutes and enjoy our cocktails and catch up with each other's news before going into the dining room shall we?" … asked Bella as she motioned for everyone to be seated.

Claudette came into the room to check the ice bucket to make sure there was plenty of ice and to see if anyone needed anything. All nodded that they were okay and Claudette turned to leave the room.

"Claudette, please advise the kitchen that we will begin dinner in 30 minutes," and Claudette nodded and exited the room.

Everyone knew the rules that no mention of a meeting/gathering was to ever occur when they were together. This was to make sure that nobody outside of the sisterhood would have any idea of their decision-making processes later after a meeting had been held. The meeting will be set up in another room that had the ability to be sealed and business conducted behind closed doors. Nobody other than the members of the sisterhood and their 2 attendants could be in the room during deliberations. The meeting is to be conducted at the end of the meal in their usual ritualistic fashion.

All the rules of the meeting were running through each of their minds as they all wanted to ask what the issue was and have an open conversation about it. However, that could NOT happen so they conducted their idle chat conversations and how are you doing discussions.

Eleanor asked Bella… "Where is David tonight? I thought we would get a chance to see him and say hello."

"Oh, David is out of town. He has a client down in New Orleans that he has to visit occasionally and that client called him to review some of his financial plans, etc. I don't follow all that stuff. Bless his heart as he will have to drive back over night to get here tomorrow as it is our anniversary. Can you believe that? We have been married 8 years already. I just don't know where the time flies," said Bella staring off into space.

"That is indeed a shame Bella, and I hope he can get home safely in order to treat you like the queen you are on your anniversary," said Eleanor.

Claudette entered the room to announce dinner is served and they all marched into the dining room to have their dinner.

After dinner Eleanor began the procession into the other room that has been prepared meticulously by Bella. Eleanor is the High Priestess of the group and takes the lead naturally. She opens the door into their meeting room and is met by 2 women who have been their attendants since the beginning. They were recruited as potential members but it was later determined that they would better serve as attendants as they did not have any evident skills to become members. They have been sworn to secrecy and have been tested and have passed. They are to be trusted.

The attendants adorned each sister with their robes. Each robe was white representing the purity of their intent but had a rope belt that was a little different color representing their individual skills and what they brought to the group.

Eleanor's belt was gold – representing her position as High Priestess and also her ability to read the auras of each sister as well as others around her. She was uncanny in her ability to know exactly someone's mood at that moment and this was particularly useful in business dealings as well. She was about 15 when she discovered this ability.

Luna's belt was Navy blue which represented her ability to freeze all action in the room if necessary. Her skill to do this was one that just appeared one day when they were all out shopping and they lost Evie and couldn't find her. Luna for whatever reason just closed her eyes and commanded everything to cease and the room froze. She opened her eyes and found that she was able to walk around everyone else who was just standing in place. She easily found Evie and blinked her eyes and woke everyone up. Nobody knew they had been frozen in place and they resumed their conversations as if nothing had happened. Luna grabbed Evie's hand and pulled her back to where the others were. When she told them about her ability later, she had to show them again and she took pictures the next time as they still didn't believe her as they didn't remember a thing.

Evie – her belt was emerald green representing her ability to see events happening in the future. This was extremely beneficial so she could understand what was happening in her real estate world. She learned how to use this talent or skill early on around her mid-teens. She was able to determine testing information in school, how things would turn out with new boyfriends, etc. She was almost perfect in her ability to forecast what was going to happen and she was asked "many" times to provide info that one of the sisters needed to know. She often called meetings in the past since she was able to see what was going to happen to one of them.

Bella – her belt was orange representing her ability to be intuitive and have clairvoyance on multiple occasions. It manifested when they had met to go to dinner one evening and then on to see a movie. During dinner Bella kept feeling strange. She felt that something was wrong and wasn't sure what it was. She knew that something was either going to happen soon or was happening at that moment.

This was all new to her and she learned over the years how to read it, but this first time almost had her sick to her stomach. She mentioned to the others that she would have to go home as she wasn't feeling well. They all decided to take her home and to cancel going on to the movie that evening.

The next morning the news showed that the theater they had been planning on attending had the popcorn machine catch on fire and the fire spreading injuring many and killing over 20 people. Bella's illness had saved them from being in the middle of that horrible situation. They never doubted her when she got one of her feelings again.

Believe it or not they were able to use their talents many times over the years to help protect each other and to have useful tools that benefitted them in their businesses.

Now that they had their robes on, they moved towards the large round wooden table in the center of the room. There were 4 high back chairs placed strategically around the table. Each sister moved to their respective chair.

There was an altar to the immediate right-hand side of the room as they entered; and it was comprised of all white candles and clear blocks. There were 4 shrines placed, one at the east, north, west and south walls of the room.

The East shrine represented Air and was shaped with wooden blocks holding green candles to remind all of spring.

The South shrine presented the element of fire and was designed in a triangle shape by bricks for a base with red and pink candles. This shrine represented summer.

The West shrine provided the water position and was represented by a wavy container and black and dark toned candles for the deep hues of water. This brought winter into the equation.

Then the North shrine was square shaped with ceramic and terra cotta pots holding orange and yellow candles. This represented the transition of seasons and brought it all together.

Eleanor had always been the high priestess of the group and the natural leader. After each sister is robed, they moved to the altar. They joined Eleanor at the entry altar after she picked up the white taper candle that was at her place at the table. She opened the ritual by lighting the white candles of the entry altar. She called the others to her side where she anointed their heads with essential oil and sage incense from the entry altar. She chanted, *"Please enlighten our minds with the truth, inspire our hearts with love, engrave our will with courage, enrich our lives with service and attract happiness and meaning into our lives".*

Each sister moved behind Eleanor after being anointed. They then followed her to each Shrine where she lit the first candle while Evie spoke the chant for that particular shrine. At the East Shrine Evie chanted *"Spring, powers of air, step forth from darkness and enter our circle as dark gives way to light"* while Eleanor lit the first candle with one white taper from the center alter. Then she passed this taper on to each sister who then lit another candle showing unity within the group.

This practice continued to the rest of the shrines with Evie chanting and Eleanor lighting the first candle and the others lighting the remaining candles and continued until all candles had been lit at all 4 shrines and the entry altar.

Each sister then returned to stand behind their high back chair at their station at the table. Eleanor then chanted; *"Those gathered in this house will hear the truth from their mouths"*, as they all nodded together.

Each sister then raised her arms out to her side towards each sister near her, as if trying to hold hands. They were too far apart to actually hold hands however, together they chanted; *"Lovelight between hands – join us and connect us as one to each other"* and once this was uttered together by all 4 sisters – sparks flew between their hands and joined them as one. This action never ceased to amaze each of them as their unity was bound together and strongly ignited by electrical charge between them.

The ritual has been opened and ready for the meaning of the gathering to be discussed. The attendants helped each sister be seated in their chair and brought them each a glass of wine of their preference. The attendants then withdrew to the back of the room until summoned to assist again.

Eleanor opened the conversation by thanking all for attending as this was a very serious situation that required all their attention.

"This is a somber moment for me to have to share this information with you." Eleanor spoke with heavy breathes. She continued, "we have spent past times overcoming issues affecting one of us for whatever reason. We are faced with another one of those issues and it affects Bella the most."

With that statement, Bella looked directly at Eleanor with a question on her face. What in the world is she talking about? She has learned over the years that if the subject of the meeting happens to affect one of the sisters in particular; that sister is to remain silent until all the facts are presented. Bella steadied herself to remain calm and silent until she heard all of the information to be presented.

The two attendants moved from the back of the room to one on each side of Bella's chair. This is done as a precaution just in case that sister needs assistance during this portion of the meeting.

Eleanor continues with her explanation. Seems that the biggest concern is going to directly affect Bella as her husband David is the reason the meeting has been called. Eleanor explains that David is moving money to a bank in the Bahamas and is sure that Bella does not know anything about this. She looks at Bella who has a very puzzled look on her face.

Eleanor explains, "A good friend of mine is at the particular bank that David is sending this money to and she called me to verify that David is who he said he was." "Apparently he didn't know that she knew me and he simply told her he was from Hamp Bayou, Mississippi and was setting up a business there and would be transferring funds from his bank in Hamp Bayou." When she told me that he was moving over $20 million US Dollars to her bank I was shocked and then began to suspect that something was going on.

She went on to say. "There was no logical reason for him to be doing that type of transaction unless he was trying to hide something, and I was pretty sure that Bella was in the dark on this."

Bella started to speak but Eleanor put up her hand and said, " I am sorry Bella, but not yet. There is more to be shared."

Eleanor went on to explain "I began to check around to see if I could figure out what was going on when I ran into another friend of mine who suggested I may want to check on David's purchasing of property in Bahama's. So I called Evie to do some checking for me. Evie nodded in acknowledgement.

Evie volunteered her contribution to the evidence being presented, "I did some checking and discovered that David purchased several parcels of land along with a single-family home there that was on the market for over 1 year and he paid full price for it. He didn't try to bargain or negotiate with the seller but seemed to buy it as a quick purchase. I told Eleanor that I thought he was trying to surprise you Bella with a home to stay at in the Bahama's and that was why he just wanted to close so quickly. However, I was floored when I got a copy of the purchase agreement sent to me by the real estate broker who is a friend of mine. That is when I called Eleanor to explain that I thought something else was going on."

Eleanor picks it back up by saying, "I then got a call from a friend of mine who explained that she had just seen David out at one of her watering holes and that David was with Anne in a rather compromising situation in the little town just south of Hamp's Bayou. She was at the bar having one of her happy hour tini's which was her custom on this particular day and she was seated at the far corner of the bar which was her favorite place to sit and watch things that happened in that bar. She watched as this couple came into the bar and moved to be seated in one of the booths at the edge of her viewing area.

"However", Eleanor explains, "she was not able to make out David very clearly and at first thought it was Bella with him as the woman looked just like you Bella. She started to raise her hand and yell hello when she realized that it was not you Bella but it was Anne your assistant. I know you two look a lot alike which fools a lot of people."

Eleanor continues… "It seems that David was holding hands with Anne and they were in deep conversation. Then David gets up from the other side of the booth and sits next to Anne and begins to kiss her and make out with her right there in the booth." I personally found this hard to believe but my friend insisted on her correctness.

My friend said she was a bit embarrassed by his carrying on with Anne like that and she almost walked over to speak to them but chose not to. Eleanor adds, "I am so sorry Bella for not telling you about this earlier but I needed to gather more information to verify this really happened.

Eleanor adds, "there is more to this story.

After further investigation, I have learned that Anne is actually related to you Bella as your stepsister." With that statement, all the sisters turned to Eleanor with gasps. What is she talking about? Eleanor continues, "It seems that your father happened to be having an affair with a woman he worked with at the factory and that woman became pregnant. Your father wanted nothing to do with that child and he threatened the woman to remain silent. He would give her money to help raise the child but he could not be present to help her as he would not leave his family. That woman agreed to only receive the child support and her child never knew her father.

This little girl grew up knowing that one day she would find her father and confront him. That little girl is Anne your assistant Bella. That is why she resembles you so much. You two have the same father." Eleanor looked at Bella with such sadness that everyone was concerned about what this information was doing to Eleanor's emotional state as well as how it was affecting Bella.

Bella bent her head down holding it in her hands as all this information was overwhelming and she just wasn't sure how to grasp it all and make any sense out of it.

Could Anne really be her sister? Could David be having an affair with Anne? How could all this be true? Her sisters have never lied to her before and her entire life seemed to be crumbling down around her. Her life was perfect in her mind and now she has learned that it has all been a lie.

Her eyes filled with tears as she fought to remain in control and felt her whole world slipping away at the same time. Her chest seemed to have a heavy weight bearing down on it and she couldn't move. She felt paralyzed with anguish and grief.

Why is David moving money to the Bahama's was the question that kept running through Bella's mind? That made no sense to her except that maybe now there was another motive. This idea seemed to break her heart in half. The excruciating pain was almost unbearable. And then the sobs began and she was out of control.

The sisters all rose together and went to her side and consoled her and to try to bring her some relief from her grief. They all had tears coming down their cheeks as the hurt Bella was feeling affected them all.

After a few minutes the sisters returned to their seats as Bella's sobs subsided. Eleanor spoke again. "This has probably been the hardest thing I have ever had to do and Bella my sweet sister, it pains me even more than words can say to have to tell you all of this but there is more. I have had my best team working on this privately and I just want you to know that I gave David the benefit of my doubt first and finally had to change my mind once I had all the facts. And the other sad fact is that Anne has been the catalyst that has orchestrated the infidelity against you with your husband and that it was intentional on her part in an effort to get even with your father. Her intent was to get your husband under her control and to have him get money control away from you and into her hands and then she would dump him once she had screwed your life up. Then she would send for her mother to leave your father and cause him additional pain as well. They would have their justice finally against your father and ultimately you."

Bella just sat there and listened intently and tried to absorb all that was being told to her. She found it more and more difficult as the pain in her chest kept mounting and she was afraid she might be having a heart attack just like her mother. She kept gasping for air and eventually caught her breath and began to settle back down into a normal breathing rhythm. This seemed to reduce the weight on her chest and the pain was subsiding a little bit.

Bella raised her hand to signal Eleanor to stop talking for a moment. She needed some time to regroup.

The sisters all understood and so did Eleanor who ceased talking and gave the floor to Bella. The attendants refreshed everyone's drinks so that they could all regroup with their thoughts and collect their emotions. No decisions could be made while everyone was in such an emotional state.

Several minutes passed and it seemed like hours to a couple of the sisters, but Bella finally had gathered herself together and began to speak. "Eleanor, I am sure this was very painful for you to have to tell me all of this and I am thankful that you had the courage to bring this to me. Having you and the rest of you on my side brings me some peace but needless to say; the pain of learning all of this is almost overwhelming. I had no idea any of this was going on and the shock alone is enough to cause great pain but the overall thought of what is happening is even more outrageous and has now caused my blood to begin to boil. There is always two sides to every story so I want to hear the other side of the story if I may before coming to a final conclusion," Bella sighed with a heavy breath. Bella continued with … "I am requesting that no action take place until I have heard the other side of the story."

Eleanor had lowered her head while Bella was talking and lifted it at the end to explain to everyone, "Bella, I totally agree that there are two sides to every story and because of that I did something else to provide the proof. I had a friend of mine befriend Anne and eventually got her to explain what was on her mind and my friend recorded it. That is how I pieced all the information together. I have the recording with me if you wish to listen to it."

With that statement, Eleanor nodded and one of the attendants brought the tape player to the table and put it in front of Bella.

Bella sat there for a few minutes staring at the tape player. She held her finger over the play button for what seemed like an eternity until she finally pushed the button.

Everything that Eleanor had said was happening became crystal clear after listening to Anne explain to the other person recording her of her plans to annihilate Bella and her father for depriving her of a decent life growing up. Anne was so angry on the tape and the revenge in her voice was deeply seated and almost scary.

All the sisters listened to the tape along with Bella. Listening to this woman who they had all grown to love over the years was hateful and vengeful and out to hurt their dear sweet Bella with everything she had. Luna shook her head back and forth as if it is just so unbelievable. Evie had her fingers clasped together as if praying that this would be over soon. There was no evidence of any emotion one way or the other with her. Luna was crying softly for Bella and Eleanor just stared at the tape player and watched the tape go round and round. She had already listened to this tape many times and knew it almost verbatim.

Do they have a plan? Not yet….

And nobody in the room was aware that there was someone else there. He had been in the garage earlier that morning when Bella left for work and had spent most of the day avoiding the housekeeper and lawn maintenance personnel. As soon as he learned of this gathering, he found a place where he could observe without being seen. He learned a great deal about Mr. David and would report what he learned to Mr. Delgado at his first chance to escape this house.

CHAPTER 6

THE PROCESS

After listening to the tape of Anne explaining gleefully how she was going to take down Bella and her stupid husband David and annihilate her father, the sisters collectively nodded to address the problem. There is a process as to how they address issues, and the affected sister is removed from the deliberation.

Eleanor looks at Bella and says "Bella my sweet sister, you know what has to happen now. You must excuse yourself from the room and let us go to work on finding a solution to this problem for you. You are not to be a part of this action for your own protection. And, as you know, you are not to speak of it to anyone. Not even David or Anne. You cannot discuss it with anyone and that includes your father. You may speak with us about it but we are not allowed to divulge what our actions are as we go forward and you are to trust in our decisions. Is that perfectly clear Bella?"

Bella nodded that she understood as she was very familiar with this part of their ritual. She had been a part of it before on multiple occasions, but this was the first time it affected her personally. Now she fully understood how difficult this was with her other sisters who had been a part of this in the past. Removing yourself from the action or decision making was very difficult but she would trust her sisters to do the right thing. They have always done what is right and the best action for the sister affected. Hard decisions have been made in the past, but the final outcome was always for the best results. They were very good at what they do, and Bella knew she had to step aside and let the process happen.

Bella slipped out of the room and went directly to the bar in her dining room and made herself a stiff drink. Her hands were shaking, and she realized that she had some major thinking to do and had to collect herself before her husband David came home from New Orleans tonight. Tomorrow as their wedding anniversary. Oh Lord, how was she going to get through that without letting on to him that she was aware of what was going on? The tears were streaming down her face as she slammed back a full glass of bourbon hoping that would settle her nerves.

Eleanor looked at the other sisters and motioned to the attendants to refill everyone's glasses. Everyone's beverages were refilled, and discussion began.

"Let's break this down and determine how we wish to move forward. Any ideas anybody?", said Eleanor as she swallowed most of her wine with one drink.

Evie says, "Give me a minute as I want to take a look to see if I can see anything in the future."

Eleanor looked at all of them and saw that everyone's aura was glowing deep blue to which she recognized as meaning they were all still emotional about the issue. She needed to get them to relax and become more balanced. She needed to get their auras to white, if at all possible, tonight.

Eleanor asked everyone to be as quiet as possible for Evie to see what the future held if she was able to do that tonight. All of them would have trouble until they quieted their emotions and went on with the process.

Luna was shaking her head saying, "This is unbelievable. We need to be careful how we proceed from here as there are a lot of people involved. I can get a couple of my investigators to check out this information to make sure all the information is accurate. Then I will check on the validity of David being able to move funds out of a joint account for that amount of money without the other signor on the account signing off. Moving thousands of dollars is one thing, but moving Millions is another. We need to find a way to get that money back into Bella's account asap."

"I will take care of that Luna. Banking is my business and I believe I know how to get this to happen," said Eleanor.

Evie spoke up by asking "Has anybody verified that Bella's father is really Anne's father? Not sure why I think this, but something is not correct; I can feel it, and possibly we need to do a paternity test somehow to confirm that. It would be a shame to think all this happened intentionally to Bella and David when it was in error."

Eleanor added, "You are correct Evie. It would be important that we somehow collect DNA from both Anne and Bella's father to verify that he is indeed the father. This must be done without them knowing it is happening as we don't want Anne to think that we know something. And as to having David be a victim. Well, all I can say is he made his bed by developing a relationship with Anne like he did. He threw the trust that Bella had for him out the window and he doesn't deserve any consideration as far as I am concerned."

Evie was stirring and everyone turned to look at her. She opened her eyes and looked at all the faces staring at her. She looked at them and said …. "I did not get a clear picture of what the future held for Bella and David. I did get a future picture of Anne who was crying in a room all by herself. I am not sure where the room was, but it was stark and clean white walls with only a table and a couple of chairs in the room. That was all I could pull from my meditation at this time.

Possibly more information tomorrow or later tonight. I think there is just too much emotion still happening for me to get a clear picture"

Eleanor knew this had been a very emotional night for all of them and that it was going to be hard to come up with a solution tonight as the sisters were trying to calm themselves to develop a good plan of action, and they all knew that they had to be calm and responsible as this will affect the future of one of their sisters.

Luna could see the struggle everyone, including Eleanor was going through. She said, "Perhaps we should determine what our first steps should be and then let's collect our evidence and then meet again to discuss further what we need to do next. My first suggestion would be to layout an action plan based on what we already know. May I suggest that I do some investigative work by having my team collect DNA samples from Anne and Bella's father."

Luna adds, "I can freeze the room while you go in and dig through his desk to get the info if you want. I am good at doing that." And everyone laughed. A good laugh to lighten the tension.

Then Evie says, "I can check on Anne's mother as I know her from the quilting club I belong to. She is a member also and I can possibly check her mind to see if I can read anything going on that way by feeding her some information and see if she responds mentally.

With these plans decided upon Eleanor says, "Okay everyone, you have your marching papers. Let's get this going and can we meet back here in 3 days with what we have collected?" Everyone nodded and they went to leave.

The 2 attendants helped each sister remove her robe and rope belt. These were hung neatly on hooks under each sister's name to the left of the door. Luna then froze the attendants to clear their memory.

As each sister left the room and entered Bella's living room where she was sitting quietly drinking another glass of bourbon. Each sister went to her individually and gave her a hug and kiss on the cheek. Eleanor whispered in her ear for her not to worry as they were investigating first before taking any action. This seemed to bring some relief to Bella.

Eleanor knew that Bella needed to not be home when David arrived from New Orleans so she pulled Bella aside and suggested that she leave town for about a week and by then things will settle down. The two of them put together a logical explanation as to why she would go out of town the eve of her wedding anniversary.

Eleanor had Luna call Bella's phone number and they let Claudette answer the phone. Luna whispered in a disguised voice to speak to Bella and Claudette brought the phone to Bella saying the call was for her.

Bella took the phone …"Hello, this is Bella".. she spoke in her sweet southern tone with a bit of tension in her voice. She as still struggling to digest all the information and was trying to hold back the tears.

"Bella, this is Luna and you are to get really upset with me and begin to cry and carry on and Eleanor will take over". And then Luna actually hung up the phone and went to Bella's side.

Bella screamed "Oh No, that is horrible" as she began to sob heavily. Claudette came running into the room to make sure Bella was okay. Eleanor put up her hand and told Claudette that the sisters had this and they would get things handled. Claudette left the room knowing that her Bella would be well taken care of as these women always took such good care of each other.

Eleanor took over the phone and relayed her sympathy to whomever was on the phone. In reality there was nobody on the other end of the phone and Eleanor was very effective in making everyone in the room believe there had been a tragedy and that Bella would have to leave immediately to go to the family of one of her dear college friends who was in a terrible accident and possibly would not survive the night.

Eleanor maneuvered Bella to go upstairs by saying …" Bella, let's get your bags packed and I will make arrangements for a flight to Dallas to leave asap". This was said loud enough for the house staff to know what was going on.

Then Eleanor whispers, "Evie, can you get copies of the real estate purchase contracts David made in Nassau? We will want to check on them to make sure signed correctly, etc.

"Of course, I can do that," said Evie.

While everyone was in the living room the two attendants cleaned up the gathering room and then left the house at the back door. Nobody saw them come in or go out. The extra visitor in the house observed this action and took the same route. His car was parked several blocks away and he would soon get to it and would be able to call his boss with an update.

CHAPTER 7

The Next 24 hours

ELEANOR/BELLA

Eleanor made a few phone calls and everything was lined up. A private jet will whisk Bella out of town immediately. She needed to be gone before David got back into the house. Everyone had played their part very well and Eleanor was sure that the house staff all understood that Bella was very upset about the emergency with her dear college friend. Eleanor got her to the plane as quickly as possible.

Eleanor also contacted some friends who owned a hotel in Dallas and arranged for a beautiful suite for Bella overlooking a scenic section of the city. She stressed to hotel owners that her friend Bella was going through a rough time and just needed some tender loving care, and she was to be given anything she wanted while she was staying there. All expenses were to be covered by Eleanor. This made Eleanor feel better to help out this way considering she was the one who brought all this grief to Bella.

Bella was instructed to totally vent and get the stress out of her system that she had learned about her husband while away. This was a perfect situation to keep her out of her home so that she would not have to face David and confront him with what she knew. She knew that she could not control herself and wasn't sure just how deep her rage would go. Eleanor saved her from having to find that out. Besides, the sisters had to devise their plan to resolve this situation. Bella was not sure just what they would do but she would accept whatever decision they came to.

ANNE

Anne arrived the next morning at the office and didn't see Bella anywhere. This was rather strange and had never occurred since she started working there. Bella was always at the office very early and would be deep in concentration on new fashion lines well before 7 in the morning. Bella was an early riser and many times just came straight to the office to get her mind geared up and motivated.

Anne decided to call Bella's home to just to see what was going on. The phone only rang a couple of times when the housekeeper Claudette picked up the phone.

"Hi Claudette, this is Anne. I haven't seen Bella this morning. Is she running late"?

Claudette answered ... "Good morning Miss Anne. Our Bella is out of town. She received an emergency phone call last night that one of her dear college friends had been in a terrible accident and was not expected to make it through the night. Ms. Eleanor made arrangements and flew Bella to Dallas last night. I am not sure when she will return."

"Oh I am so sorry to hear that. Please let me know if there is anything I can do to help" was Anne's reply as a large grin spread across her face. What a lucky day this is going to be for her. She hung up the phone and just sat there spinning around in the chair grinning from ear to ear. The Queen is gone and I am in charge was her mantra for the day and she took a minute to revel in that thought and then called her mother.

DAVID

David had driven to New Orleans and found that the drive back was a real pain. He didn't want to leave New Orleans but knew he had to get home as it was his wedding anniversary to Bella. He knew she would be expecting him to have planned something special. He would have to get all that figured out tomorrow as he couldn't concentrate on anything while driving other than the special 3 days he had just experienced in New Orleans.

David pulled up in front of their home and found it to be rather dark considering that it wasn't that late. He had actually arrived an hour after Eleanor got Bella on a plane and flew her away from Hamp's Bayou.

He parked his car in his usual spot and grabbed his bag from the trunk and headed to the house. When he opened the front door, he saw Claudette cleaning in the living room. He stuck his head in the room and said…" Hi Claudette. You are working late. Where is Bella?"

"Oh Mr. David. I am just cleaning up after Ms. Bella's dinner party with her sisters. She had to leave to go out of town as one of her dear friends from college had been in some sort of terrible accident. The family called Ms. Bella to join them as her friend may not make it through the night. Ms. Eleanor arranged to fly Ms. Bella to Dallas right away. They left about an hour ago." Claudette provided a thorough explanation and felt confident she had done the right thing.

"Oh, I see. Thanks Claudette. I will give her a call in a bit to check up on her and see how thing are going. I am headed upstairs and will retire now. Thank you and don't work too late. This can wait until tomorrow if you wish" … said David in a matter-of-fact tone.

David went upstairs carrying his luggage and was happy to know he had time to remove all his clothing and potentially get rid of any residual evidence of being with another woman that he may have overlooked. He plopped down on the king size bed and just laid there smiling thinking about what a magnificent time he had in New Orleans. He felt lucky to have been able to spend time with Anne who truly did know how to please a man. He fell asleep fully dressed as he was totally exhausted.

The next morning David woke up and realized he was still dressed. He called downstairs and asked Claudette to bring him some coffee and toast with butter and honey. He then jumped in the shower to get himself going for the day. With Bella gone he felt liberated and pumped full of energy. He hadn't felt this good in who knows how long. He felt fantastic.

When he came out of the shower, he found the coffee and toast that Claudette had brought up for him. He felt he needed to call Bella and check up on the current situation. He wanted to check up and see how things were going. When he dialed her cell phone, he heard it ring. She had left her cell phone on her personal nightstand. This was not like Bella at all so he thought this must have really been an emotional moment for her to leave her cell phone behind. He would contact Eleanor later to find out how to reach his wife.

Fixing his coffee with a drop of cream he just pondered for moment, how the rest of his day would go. But first, he would have to get dressed and go see his newly established love interest and check on her. He couldn't wait to see Anne. He wondered if Anne knew that Bella was out of town.

ELEANOR

Eleanor had a hard time getting any sleep that night. It had all been so emotional. And, getting Bella out of town before David got home had been a pretty close call considering nobody really knew when David was due to arrive.

Eleanor knew she had to make a personal call to one of her friends in the Inspector Generals Office. She called her friend Carol Johnson who was an old college classmate. They had kept in contact with one another over the years. Carol had been helpful to Eleanor in the past and Eleanor was hoping she would find the information she had beneficial.

"Inspector General's Office, DC Branch, Investigator Johnson here. How can I help you?" … said Carol in a very professional manner.

"Hey Carol, it's Eleanor Hicks from Hamp's Bayou, Mississippi calling." announced Eleanor in her professional manner.

Both laughed and said their hellos in a much more familiar way. The Eleanor got down to business quickly. She explained what was happening and wondered if this was something that Carol would be interest in.

"This is totally in my realm of responsibility. As an investigator with the IG Office we have been keeping our eyes and ears open to find these types of perps. I thank you for turning me on to this creep. Send me his details and we will take it from there," said Carol.

Eleanor agreed to forward the details she had to date on to Carol. They ended the conversation with their usual we need to get together and catch up with one another lines knowing full well that will never happen.

After hanging up with Carol, Eleanor sat down at her computer and gather all the information she could muster and sent it to Carol's email. Then she made a note to herself to call Luna and check on her progress.

Eleanor then called David's bank in Nassau, Bahamas and asked for the owner. She would get more response with an owner rather than a teller or bank manager. They were a dime a dozen, but she had more clout with dealing with owners of any establishment. Explaining that her client was David Thomas who happened to open an account there a few days prior and his wife needed to have a signature card on file for future use. Could he please send her the signature cards necessary and she would personally take care of getting this taken care of asap?

The owner was very accommodating, and Eleanor thought that he felt more assured since he was dealing with the bank owner of the account that transferred over $20 million dollars to an account at his bank. He agreed to send the signature cards directly to her business email address to which Eleanor agreed to have back to him by the end of the day.

LUNA

Luna sprung out of bed like there was a bomb ready to go off. She had no idea what caused her to do that except she was compelled to get things rolling on her investigation. She was going to get this wrapped up asap.

First things first, she called John and Eddie (her investigators) and asked them to meet her first thing in her office. Today was one of those days that she was very happy to have these two guys working for her. They have been very beneficial to her in the past but now this was critical for Bella and she needs them to be on their best. She would go over all the details with them when she saw them.

The phone rang and it was Eleanor. "Good morning sunshine. Hope you managed to get some sleep Luna" … said Eleanor with a genuine concern.

Luna said…" I did okay but could have slept better. That was a tough night and many things were rolling around in my head all night. I am meeting with my investigators when I get to the office. I will get the DNA tests done asap, also going to get some surveillance camera's up in strategic places and will have David followed as well as that little bitch Anne. We will know their every move. Have you spoken to Bella this morning Eleanor? I am so very worried about her." Added Luna with a heavy sigh.

"I have a call into her and hopefully will get to talk with her this morning. There are some things she needs to do for me, so I hope to talk with her before lunch. Is there something you need me to discuss with her for you?" asked Eleanor.

"No Eleanor, I have it covered. My goal is to have verified the DNA by tomorrow the latest and have some additional information on the relationship side by the end of today. I hope to speak to my partners as to the validity of the bank account without Bella's authorization to move the money, etc."

"Oh wait, don't worry about that" … said Eleanor, " because I spoke with the bank in Nassau and they are sending signature cards so I can have Bella sign and get back to them. Once that is done, we can move money around wherever we want. That is something we can get done asap and get that money back into Bella's control."

With that being said both Luna and Eleanor were happy to have some forward progress for Bella's sake.

Luna hung up the phone after finishing the conversation with Eleanor. She promptly got dressed and headed to her office. Both John and Eddie were sitting there waiting on her when she arrived. She grabbed a cup of black coffee from the kitchen and then marched into her office and motioned for both men to join her. She motioned for Eddie to close the office door behind them.

"Gentlemen, thank you for being here so promptly. I have a task for you that I am putting you on in total confidence. And it is to be top priority with 100% secrecy. I have a dear friend who has a bastard for a husband who is fooling around on her. I want some surveillance cameras in these locations" … said Luna as she passed the list over to John and Eddie.

"I want him followed 24/7 and you can take turns doing that. I want to know his every move. I also want to know his girlfriends every move." She added with a strong hand bang on her desk.

"Oh, and there is another thing. I need a DNA sample from two people on this list. You will need to get samples somehow, discretely for sure, and I will give you all the details about each person. I want the

DNA samples in the lab by tonight so we can get the results tomorrow morning. This is critical and time is of the essence" … stated Luna, driving the point home.

Both men knew she meant business and their jobs could be on the line if they didn't get this work done just like she wanted.

"Ok boss. We are outta here. We will take it from here. No worries" said Eddie as he and John bounced out of Luna's office.

JOHN & EDDIE

Both men knew that their boss was pretty uptight about this new project she had them working on. They knew they better perform or they would not have a job. So, John immediately called some friends of his that owned surveillance equipment and spoke to them about placing some cameras in strategic locations without anyone knowing. His friends were up to the task and they were immediately deployed to get that going. John found the fax machine and sent his friends the list of the locations for the cameras.

Eddie knew too that they had to be on their best game to pull all this off in 24 hours. He was hoping that the DNA subjects would be easy to get to. They agreed that in order to get this accomplished by tonight they had to split up. They did a coin flip as to who got who. Eddie drew heads and he got Anne and John got what was left and he got some old guy. This was all a little weird but it was not their position to understand anything. They just had to get the job done.

John's friends were already on their way to place the cameras according to the list he had faxed over. They have done this type of thing before and felt very comfortable entering establishments and putting cameras in place without being seen or detected. The actual surveillance equipment will be set up in their office and when ready John and Eddie can come by to watch whatever it is that they are looking for on the film.

BELLA

Bella felt stiff and ached all over. She had cried herself to sleep and still found herself pulsing with rage even after crying herself into exhaustion. She knew she would have to talk to Eleanor this morning, but she dreaded it because it brought everything back to the surface and she was desperately trying to drown it all out of existence.

She sat up in the bed and looked around at her surroundings. This was a beautiful room and she had been lucky that Eleanor knew the owners as they escorted her thru the back entrances and kept her presence a secret to anyone who might be watching. The view with the floor to ceiling windows was spectacular, especially at night as she remembered it slightly upon her arrival last night. Her eyes were burning from all the crying, but she recalled seeing all the incredible city lights of Dallas from her room and thought under different circumstances this would have been a perfect romantic encounter.

The little red light on her bedside phone was blinking and Bella instantly knew there was a message for her. She reached over and picked up the phone to retrieve the message. She listened to Eleanor's message. She is to call her at her earliest convenience. Bella sighed and slipped out of bed and headed to the shower.

The hot water hit her skin and she felt her muscles relaxing. She had no idea just how tense she had been over the past 12 hours or so. She just stood there letting the hot water soothe her and bring her some relief. Eventually she turned the water off and reached for the towel outside the shower and wrapped herself in the comfort of this very soft, oversized towel. These hotel owners sure know how to make their guests feel special.

She picked up the phone and called for room service and asked to have some coffee and a bran muffin brought to her room. She was beginning to get a little hungry and a bran muffin sounded perfect this morning. She opened her suitcase and pulled out some slacks and a top. She got herself dressed quickly so that she was ready when room service showed up with her coffee. She would call Eleanor after she had a cup of coffee in her.

Room service was extremely efficient and delivered her coffee and a plate full of bran muffins along with some fresh fruit. Bella was beginning to regroup and gather herself. She was so glad that Eleanor got her out of Hamp's Bayou. She knew it would have been a very bad scene if she had stayed there and confronted David. That bastard. How could he?

She was also glad that Eleanor made her leave her cell phone at home as David would have no way of reaching her and she could remain totally removed from whatever was going on back in Hamp's Bayou. She didn't want to know any of it and wasn't sure if she would even return to the Bayou. All of this was so embarrassing.

She picked up the phone and dialed Eleanor who answered on the first ring. "Hi Bella... how are you doing this morning?" ... asked Eleanor in her sweetest southern charm.

"I am hanging in there Eleanor" ... said Bella. "I have managed to get a shower, had a cup of coffee and muffin and now I am wondering what in the world I am going to do the rest of today."

Eleanor chimed in... "Oh I have some chores for you to do today. I will be sending some signature cards for you to sign and have the front desk at the hotel scan them and return to me as soon as you get them. This is to make sure we get the money that is in the Nassau account back into your possession." Eleanor stressed the importance of getting them signed and returned immediately.

"Ok Eleanor" .... whispered Bella. "Just send me the instructions on what you want me to do and I will get it done for you today. I understand that this is important. I also understand that we must be aware of time constraints. I just don't want to know too many details" … and with that Eleanor agreed and they hung up the phone.

BELLA's FATHER - Charlie

Charlie was enjoying his morning coffee when he got a call from his new lady friend. Well, she wasn't really a new lady friend. He had been with her before and she had managed to be so careless and become pregnant. He had been so surprised when she resurfaced into his life after Margie, his wife passed away. He had met the child he had fathered one day at his daughter's office. She was now working for his precious Bella. She seemed charming enough and didn't know that he was her father. He was thankful for that as he had no intention of telling Bella or his sons that they had a stepsister. He would never take a chance to diminish his family relationship with this type of ugly news.

Well Candice, Anne's mother, had called him to discuss their plans for dinner that evening. He had asked her to go out to dinner with him and then on to a movie or some other type of entertainment. She needed to know the time and dress code so that she could plan accordingly. "I want to make sure I dress appropriately for you and make this a special occasion sweetie", she purred into the phone.

For whatever reason he found this type of conversation annoying. He had only wanted to take her to dinner and it was not to be anything special. She always took things the wrong way and he wasn't sure just how much more of this he would be willing to endure with her. He could kick himself for even getting involved with her again. He broke it off once before and thought it was over. Then she began coming by with food and offered him some condolences and it helped him through his grief. He felt so dumb getting involved with her again and now Anne, her daughter is getting closer and closer to his Bella. He didn't like that at all. He also needed to consider that the longer he was with her, the closer his family gets to finding out who Anne is and he most definitely did not want that to happen.

He told her where they were going to dinner and that he was not going to be able to do anything else except dinner and he hoped she understood. She said she did and he hung up the phone with a heavy sigh. This was becoming too cumbersome for him and he was going to have to end it. He was concerned because if he made her mad, she may tell his kids about Anne. He had to be extra careful and make it look like she broke up with him. He had to plan this perfectly. He had to get her really mad at him and he would have to plan this very carefully.

He decided to go to the grocery store and stock up on a few things. He had learned to do all these household chores when Margie got sick and he had to take over these chores that she normally did. He found that he really didn't mind, and it was able to decide on his dinner meals and he even learned to cook a few things. He was constantly calling Claudette at Bella's house for advice on how to make a dish a certain way. He learned a lot from Bella's house staff. They had taught him well. He was so very happy that his baby girl was now living back in Hamp's Bayou and he could see her just about any time he wanted.

Grabbing a bottle of water out of the refrigerator he headed out to do his errands and do some grocery shopping. It was a beautiful sunny day and he felt good about being healthy enough to do all the things he wanted to do at his age and that his personal health was pretty good. His doctor had told him that he was in very good shape for a man in his 70's and this was excellent news as far as he was concerned. He wasn't ready to give up the ghost yet and planned on living for many more years and enjoying his family.

He hit the cleaners first and picked up his sport coat that he dropped off last week. Then he headed to the grocery store with his list in hand. He entered the store and completed his rounds gathering up all his items in less than 20 minutes. He never bought anything unless it was on his list and he had become a very frugal shopper. He knew the aisles and where all his items were. He even did his shopping list based on the items position in each aisle. He was very proficient and had it down to a system. He took great pride in that knowledge.

He left the grocery store and emptied his cart of groceries into the trunk of his car. He had some cold products, so he had to go directly home to keep them cold. He climbed in the driver's seat and immediately reached for his water bottle and it wasn't there. He looked on the floor on the passenger side and on his driver's side and he couldn't find it. He sat there for a minute and could have sworn he left the water bottle in the holder on the console of his car like he always did. What in the world happened to it? This was a baffling thing but then he thought, maybe I am losing it today and I dumped it in the trash on the way into the grocery. Oh well, time to get these groceries home.

Nobody saw a man take that water bottle out of Charlie's car just before he returned with his groceries.

CAROL JOHNSON

Carol had called a team meeting after talking with her contact from Mississippi. The room was filling up with her team. Eleanor was a good college friend and she had provided her with information in the past but this lead was top drawer and right where all the energies of her department have recently been focusing.

"Ok everyone, listen up. I just got a great lead that I know to be dependable. I want this individual investigated with everything this department has. He has already syphoned about $20 million dollars of his wife's money out of country and my contact thinks that his financial planning business could potentially be a Ponzi scheme worth over $100 Million that may also get out of this country soon if we don't act quickly. Many innocent people's life savings are at stake and I want this guy caught yesterday. Grab a data sheet off the table and let's get to work. All info is to come to me as soon as you have any info" said Carol with her authoritative voice.

Everyone scattered and went to their desks to begin their research. It didn't take long before information came into Carol who had already set up her evidence board. She had contacted the judge to get a warrant to search David's home and to freeze his accounts. She wanted to make sure she secured as much of the money as possible so less people will be affected. The perfect case would be that nobody gets hurt and she could get him in jail before doing that to anyone. But these things never work out that way.

Carol called two of her top people into her office. "Listen you two, I am sending you to Hamp's Bayou, Mississippi to search this perp's home. I want you to confiscate any computers and files that may contain investor information. Before you make that trip understand that this may tip him off that he is under investigation. He may take off with the remaining money so do NOT... and I repeat…DO NOT go to his home until I have given you the orders". Her top team knew she meant business with this order and they intended to do as told. She always lived by the book and has never lost a case. They loved working with her as she knew how to get it done. If she says wait until she gives the order, then that is exactly what they intend to do.

DAVID

The morning was slipping away and he has not seen Anne yet today. He needed his Anne fix and jumped in his car and drove to her office. He came through the front door and saw her standing there deep in thought and looking at a piece of paper in her hand.

He slipped quietly across the room and moved in behind Anne. She had no idea he was even there as her concentration was deep.

"Ummm, you smell luscious" he whispered into her ear. Anne jumped as this startled her. She started to look around to see if anyone saw him doing this in his wife's office. Just not cool.

"What are you doing?" Anne exclaimed as she jumped back away from him. Does this idiot not have any sense at all? How could he be so unconscious with his actions. Surely, he knows what it would cost him if he let anyone see this behavior.

"It's okay. Bella is out of town and I locked the front door when I came in so that nobody can surprise us," said David as he was kissing her neck. Anne allowed him to continue as she knew she was sinking her claws into him deeper and deeper now. She needed to get him to do something today that will bring all this to an end finally.

"Honey, that feels so good and I am so happy you are here…. BUT…I need to talk to you. Can you stop for a moment and talk with me," she purred? David stopped kissing her neck and looked deeply into her eyes and knew she meant business.

"Of course my darling. I am all yours. What is on your mind?" he offered as he moved away and sat down in a chair behind the desk she always occupied.

"David darling, do you love me? Do you truly love me? Are you willing to prove it?" she asked him as she stared at him intently. She continues…." I know you have not been happy with Bella and I know that you and I are so well blended. What do you say that you and I find a way to escape all of this once and for all? You have moved some money to the Nassau account so we could start with that and begin a new life there in Nassau. What do you think?"

"What are you saying Anne? You think I should leave Bella and go with you to Nassau and that we start a new life there?" said David totally surprised at this conversation.

"Look, I know you can't do that quickly, so I have a plan worked out in my head that I want to run past you and see what you think. I want to be with you, to make you happy. To be the woman you so rightly deserve who knows how to satisfy your physical and emotional needs. We would be happy together and I think that we just need to make sure we plan it perfectly so that everything will work out the right way for everyone." She offered David as the hook goes in deeper.

Smiling, David says…"Ok sweetness, tell me your plan and let me see what you have on that pretty brain of yours."

Anne goes over to him and kisses him deeply and then sits down on his lap and begins to explain her plan.

"I think we should go to the Bahamas and you get me on your bank account so I feel you really mean business to leave Bella and be with me. Once that is done, we come back here and make arrangements to get all accounts cleared out and move additional remaining funds over to the Nassau account. Then we sit Bella down and tell her everything that is going on. That we are in love. She is going to be hurt but will know that it will be better to let you go rather than try to save a marriage that even she knows has been strained recently. Then we can plan our departure once all the legal paperwork is done for the divorce. I will feel more comfortable that I can become the new Mrs. David Thomas. So what do you think sweetie?"

David was studying her intently and determined she was indeed very serious. He had to admit that her idea wasn't a bad one but he really didn't want to hurt Bella, but he also knew that no matter what happened she was going to be hurt. His emotional attachment to Anne was so deep now he had to commit to Anne and let Bella know. This would be a difficult thing to do but Anne was right, they needed to do it the right way.

"It is a good plan and will let us be honest with Bella so that when it is over, we at least were honest with her from the beginning", he offered Anne.

"Well, not from the beginning but we will at least be as honest as can be now that we know how we feel about one another." Said Anne as sincerely as possible.

"Ok, Bella is out of town for a few days so now is a good time for you and me to head to Nassau and get me on the account and then we can slip back here, and Bella will never know we were gone. What do you think?" Anne asked David.

"Sounds good and you are right as it appears this is kismet and destined for us with her out of town like this. It is perfect for us to begin to line this up. Let's see when the next flight to Nassau is" said David as he reached for his cell phone to book a flight for them both. "This will be another great little get away for us both. Now, I am getting excited all over again", laughed David as he reached the booking agent he always used.

Within 5 minutes David had them lined up to fly to Nassau at 3:30 tomorrow afternoon as that was the earliest flight out. That would give them some time to get packed and make arrangements to be gone. They would have to travel to the airport separately as you never know who is going to see you. David was sorry he didn't book separate flights but then decided it was ending soon, so it didn't make much difference now.

David needed to see what all needed to be done to move more money out of his account in NYC to his Nassau account. He knew that once he did this, he would be dangerously close to embezzlement.

He was relatively sure he could find a place for he and Anne to live very well with this money and they could be very happy. He also knows his license would be revoked for doing this type of transaction but he wouldn't need to worry about working anymore. He did feel bad about using Bella's money, but he was going to make sure he got it back to her once they were settled. He knew that he and Anne would be living the life they both wanted. Bella had earned that money herself during her modeling career and he knew she would be furious if he took it without her permission. So, he would find a way to get it back to her. Yes, she will be very angry with him but then she will settle down once her account got stacked up again. She still had a lot of potential to earn it again if she needed to.

David left the office and drove back home. He needed to pack again and didn't want the house staff to really know where he was going so, he waited until the last minute to pack his suitcase by himself. He would find the right time to get his overnight bag to the car without too many eyes watching. Wow. Was he really doing this? And then he broke out into a huge grin. Life is sure being good to him.

ANNE

The day was turning out to be so much better than she originally thought when she found out Bella was out of town. Manipulating David was so easy it was scary. She really had been successful in wrapping him right around her little finger. This was so much easier than she thought. Could it be that tomorrow is one day closer to her redemption day? She had to get her mother brought up to speed. This was going to happen fast.

She closed the office for the day and headed home. She emptied out some garbage out of her car first that was starting to smell. Must be from last week when she ran through a fast-food place and didn't finish her sandwich. She would stop by her mother's house to bring her up to speed on the latest.

When she pulled up in the driveway, she noticed her mother's car was not there. Then she remembered that her mother told her that she was going to dinner with Charlie, Bella's father (and hers) but nobody knew that. That just made her blood boil to think about it, but she knew she was one day closer to getting even with him after all these years.

Anne thought she would just leave a note on the kitchen table for her mother to call her when she got home. She wrote that it was important and hopefully her mother would recognize the urgency and call her later that night when she got home.

She left and drove home. She was not aware of the dark sedan that had been following her all day.

When she got home, she began to pull out what clothing she was going to take to Nassau. Was this really happening tomorrow? Yes, indeed it was, and she was dancing around her bedroom with the sheer joy that her dream goal was about to happen.

She opened a bottle of wine she had chilling in the refrigerator and poured herself a tall glass.

How many years has she been planning this and now it is here? She actually hugged herself and proceeded to put her things in her overnight bag. She gathered a couple of sexy lingerie items and included them as she might as well have some intimate fun. Who knows when that will happen again? Laughing to herself she closed the case and carried it out to her car.

Later than evening, her mother called her, and Anne explained everything that was going on. She told her mother to be packed and ready to go. And to be sure to have her passport handy as they may be moving to Italy within the next couple of days. Anne detected some reluctance on her mother's part but made sure her mother knew that this was their plan and she had to be ready when the time came. That time was NOW. Her mother agreed and said she would be ready.

Anne settled in for the evening and had a very hard time getting to sleep. She laid there in bed just thinking about how easy this was going to be and how very soon she would have her revenge and would go on to have a stress-free life with her mother in another country. Living like queens. They would be so happy.

LUNA

Eddie and John contacted Luna to advise her that they had samples of the DNA from the 2 subjects in the lab and would have paternity results back within the hour. Additionally, they had surveillance cameras in the locations she had specified, and they had some information for her as to David and Anne going to Nassau tomorrow at 3:30. They had a concern as David has been checking on his bank accounts and they thought that more money may be headed to the Bahamas.

Luna was glad to get all this information and she promptly called Eleanor.

"I have an update Eleanor", said Luna as soon as Eleanor answered her phone.

She explained that she would know the paternity info within the hour and that her investigators learned that David and Anne were headed to Nassau tomorrow and there was some fear that more money would be headed to Bahamas. She explained that the surveillance she had on Anne and David proved very valuable as now she understood the actions they had planned. It was Anne's intent to be on the account and needed David there to get on the account and she lured him into the trip and getting her on the account. She then enticed him into believing she would be spending the rest of her life with him when in fact it was the farthest thing from her mind.

"And Eleanor, they intend to tell Bella that they are in love and David is going to divorce Bella," said Luna with a heavy sigh.

"Now Luna, I doubt that David will get much of a chance where he is going to worry about getting a divorce much less believe he is going to be spending the rest of his life in luxury in the arms of that slut Anne. Trust me. He is in for a rude awakening very soon!" Said Eleanor in a matter-of-fact way.

Luna totally trusted everything Eleanor ever said. She was always a straight shooter and always watched what she said and never said anything that wasn't true. This led Luna to believe that Eleanor has brought in some reinforcement outside of their group. Whatever or whomever it was, would be fine with Luna and she was sure the others will accept anything Eleanor did as gospel so no worries there.

"Luna, I think we need to regroup tomorrow night to bring everyone up to speed on where we are. We may have everything taken care of by then and I will be at liberty to privately explain more with the sisters. With Bella out of town, can you take care of contacting Claudette to prepare our meeting room for a regroup meeting. David will be gone so we won't have him sneaking around.

"Sure Eleanor," said Luna and once they hung up the phone, Luna called Claudette immediately to get the arrangements set up for 8:00 pm tomorrow night.

BELLA

The view from the hotel room windows of downtown Dallas was spectacular during the day but at night it was amazing. Bella spent the entire day laying around with ice on her eyes to help reduce the swelling caused by all her crying. The swelling seemed to be going down, but Bella kept tearing up every time she thought about what was happening. The ice may be a futile effort on her part, but she kept trying anyway.

She was wondering what was going on and what David thought since she wasn't home, and it was their wedding anniversary. Would he be upset with her and then she stopped herself. How could he be upset with me when he is the one that has broken our trust. And with this renewed anger she fueled her resolve to maintain her patience for now and get her revenge later. And, then of course, there were the sisters. They were handling things and she knew that whatever was happening they were taking care of business. She trusted them with everything she had, and she was grateful that she had them.

CAROL

The plane landed in Nassau and Carol was met by her local OIG branch members with backup support from the local officials. They briefed her on the way to her hotel that all the parties had been contacted and that everything was in order. The plan will be executed as directed. Carol was thankful to have a competent team there.

Carol called her team in Hamp's Bayou to bring them up to speed. "You are to go to the address I gave you tomorrow afternoon around 4:00 p.m. and confiscate the computer and any records that you can find and bring back to DC. Do not answer any questions or give any statements to anyone. Is this clear?" she demanded. The response was a resounding yes. Everyone understood explicitly.

After giving her Hamp's Bayou team some additional last-minute instructions, she decided to try and get some sleep since she didn't get any the night before. It was catching up with her and she wanted to be at her best tomorrow.

ANNE/DAVID

Anne was the first to leave for the airport and David followed about 20 minutes later.

Anne went through the security checks and proceeded to the gate and positioned herself where David could see her when he arrived. She managed to save a seat next to her for him.

David parked in the short-term parking lot at the airport and proceeded to the ticket counter. He forgot his ticket at home and needed another one as there was no time to go back home to get it. They issued him another ticket and he proceeded on through the security check in area. He headed on to the departure gate. There he found Anne and made a big deal about running in to her there.

"Isn't this a funny coincidence" he chuckled as he proceeded to sit down next to her.

About an hour later they were aboard the plane and were rolling down the tarmac preparing for take-off. Both were grinning from ear to ear with excitement and they had no idea what was about to happen to them.

ELEANOR

This night was a bit better than the previous night, but Eleanor didn't get much sleep again. She was nervous in the fact that some of the things she was planning were out of her control and she didn't know how it would all come down. She just had to trust that her friend had it handled and she would hear soon enough.

Luna called her with the paternity test results. "Eleanor, we have the results back," she said.

And Eleanor says, "Well are you going to share with me or what?"

Luna stutters, "But of course. Bella's father is NOT Anne's father." "We now know that for a fact," stated Luna.

Eleanor was relieved to know that they could tell Bella for a fact, that her father was NOT Anne's father and that Anne had it all wrong. Seems Anne's mother was lying about this and that now Eleanor would need to find out the true information so these rumors will cease going forward. It was just an uncanny coincidence that Anne and Bella resembled each other so closely. Eleanor thought she needed to sit down with Anne's mother and see what she could find out once and for all about this situation.

"Thank you, Luna, for letting me know this," said Eleanor as she bid Luna good night. "We will talk tomorrow night," said Eleanor as she hung up the phone and prepared herself for bed. A lot had transpired through today and Eleanor needed to regroup and gather all her information together so she could report to the sisters all that had happened along with what the outcomes were. It was going to be a very interesting meeting to say the least.

CHAPTER 8

Life Changing Events

Carol was out of bed while it was still dark outside as she was anticipating her day. She rang room service to send her up some coffee and breakfast. She felt she could eat something this morning as she wasn't sure when she would get to eat again later in the day. She jumped in the shower and was dressed before room service arrived.

She was enjoying a leisure cup of coffee when her cell phone rang. "Hello, Inspector Johnson here," she answered.

"Hi Carol, it is Eleanor Becks in Hamp's Bayou calling," said Eleanor and then added "I hope I didn't call to early".

"Not at all Eleanor," said Carol. "I am just enjoying a cup of coffee before I take off to begin my day. What's up in your world today, Eleanor?" asked Carol.

"I just wanted to bring you up to speed on what I have learned about the party I called you about a couple of days ago." said Eleanor.

"Go ahead," said Carol as she was quite interested in whatever Eleanor had to say. Eleanor then briefed Carol on the paternity info and that there was some concern about additional funds being wired to the Nassau account either today or tomorrow. She wasn't sure of the timing and it may have already happened. However, she had managed to pull funds out yesterday that belonged to her dear friend who was a victim in this case. She got those funds moved back to a Hamp's Bayou bank account so her friend was secure, but the husband was about to embezzle funds of others with any kind of transfer of funds. Eleanor felt this was vital information for Carol.

Carol thanked her and said it was indeed vital information and she would take it from there.

Carol picked up her cell phone and called her field office. There she spoke to the lead inspector and brought him up to speed. She asked him to check with the bank on any transfers either recent, within the past 24 hours or those that were pending arrival that the bank would be aware of. He agreed and would get back to her shortly. He personally knew the bank President and could get the info she requested.

Carol proceeded to eat her breakfast which was a little on the cold side but she didn't care. She felt good about how this day was going to go and that she would have another notch in her belt of catching another scum bag embezzler. Completing her breakfast, she left for the field office. Time to get this show on the road.

Eleanor had been up several hours before she called Carol with her update. Eleanor knew that today was going to be a very interesting day, but she just wasn't sure just how interesting. She did not know that Carol was in Nassau when she called her, but she felt that Carol was in total control of the situation. This pleased Eleanor as her primary goal was to get David arrested however that could happen. Little did Eleanor know that Carol was there to personally handle this situation herself.

David had managed to slip into Anne's room unnoticed by anyone sometime around 1 o'clock that morning and they had a pleasant reunion. The morning sun was starting to beam down through the curtains in the room. David could tell by peeking out through the split in the curtains, that it was going to be a beautiful day today in more ways than one.

Anne began to stir and saw David standing there by the window. She smiled and looked at him as he was staring out into the room deep in his mental thought. She wondered what he was thinking about and asked him… "Penny for your thoughts sweetie."

"Oh, I was thinking about how angry Bella will be when we tell her about us," said David pensively.

"But you know it is the right thing to do don't you honey," said Anne. David nodded and agreed with Anne and then he made passionate love to Anne as that was all that was on his mind at that moment.

Bella had finally fallen asleep somewhere around 2 that morning. She had pretty much cried all day and was exhausted from all the emotion she had been feeling. She fell into a deep troubled sleep that had her dreaming of David and their special times together and that something kept happening in her dreams that split them apart. It was frustrating Bella until she finally woke up to the sun streaming in through the curtains in her hotel suite. It took her a couple of minutes to regroup and realize where she was and why she was there. It all came screaming back into her memory and she began to tear up again. This time it wasn't quite so wrenching and she was able to control it somewhat.

She looked at the clock and saw that it was nearly 8 o'clock in the morning and Bella couldn't remember ever sleeping that long. Guess she was wiped out from the day before. Funny how she still felt exhausted but knew that things would get better with time. She just wasn't sure how she was going to get through this all with her sanity.

I have got to talk to Eleanor so she sat up in her bed and reached for her cell phone when she realized she left it at home. She then reached for the hotel phone on her nightstand. She dialed Eleanor from memory. It was easy to remember Eleanor's phone number as she had been calling her at that number for over 40 years.

"Good morning sunshine," said Eleanor as she saw the Texas number on her phone. It could only be Bella calling.

"Good morning to you Eleanor," said Bella in her soft voice.

"Did you manage to get any sleep last night?" asked Eleanor.

"Yes, I got some. Not much but I managed to eke out some rest through the night," said Bella. "I am wondering when I can come home. I have some things I need to get done and I want to be home in my own house." Said Bella.

"I know Bella," said Eleanor. "Just a little more patience my friend. We need another couple of days and then you can come on home. It will soon all be over," said Eleanor assuring Bella that they were nearing resolution.

Bella hung up the phone feeling a little bit better but a little uneasy as she had no idea what was happening but knew that Eleanor was in charge and had things covered. She just needed to remain patient and everything would be revealed to her later. So, she began to think about what she could do with her day as she could not stay in that hotel room another day. She was going to enjoy that beautiful day outside somehow.

Evie had arrived at her office early that morning as she was waiting on those documents to come in from Nassau. She got there a little after 7 that morning and found them sitting in her fax machine. She pulled them off the machine and carried them to her desk and she sat down to review them. Yes, they were the copies of the real estate sales purchase agreements for property in Nassau, Bahamas. The buyers were David Thomas and Anne Thomas. Her eyebrows raised at the Anne Thomas signature. It almost looked like Bella's signature. And, besides, when did she change her last name? Evie found this all fascinating. How could Anne have signed these papers unless she and David made the arrangements for her to fly over there to sign them when he was there before. How long has this relationship been going on without anyone knowing about it? This has made Evie furious for Bella and for the way all this was panning out.

Evie called Eleanor and arranged to bring the documents to Eleanor's office in a couple of hours once Eleanor got there. Eleanor had an appointment away from her office and wouldn't get there until after 10 that morning. Evie is to tell nobody about the documents and that Eleanor would see her that evening at Bella's house for the regroup meeting. Evie agreed and said she would see her later that morning when she dropped the papers off. Evie hung up the phone and put the papers in an envelope and sealed it. She went to the kitchen at her office and made herself a cup of Earl Grey and waited until it was time to go to Eleanor's office.

Luna was staring at her coffee cup while thinking about how much more she would learn tonight at the regroup meeting. She looked up and out her office window to enjoy the beautiful blue sky and then she saw Eleanor leaving her office and jumping in her car heading out somewhere. She wondered where she was going in such a hurry.

Candice had been up most of the night trying to decide what to pack as it might be the last time she would be here. She didn't want to leave anything behind that she really wanted. It was becoming increasingly hard to get everything to fit into a couple of suitcases. Some things were not going to make it and she was having a hard time deciding on what she really wanted.

Candice was getting worried. Eleanor Becks had called her that morning around 730 and asked if she could stop by to visit with her for a few minutes. She couldn't figure out what Eleanor Becks wanted. She hardly knew this woman and why would she want to visit with her? This had her confused and bewildered.

She looked around her little place and made sure it was neat and clean for when Eleanor arrived. She didn't want anything to look out of place. She hid her suitcases in the closet in the bedroom. Everything looked neat and straight and she was proud of herself in looking like she was in total control.

The front doorbell rang. That had to be Eleanor. Only guests used the front door. She walked to the front of her house and found Eleanor standing outside on the porch. She opened the door and said "Good Morning Ms. Becks. How are you this beautiful day?" and with that she showed Eleanor inside. She motioned for her to go to the back of the house to the kitchen where she had some coffee brewing and some Danishes on the table.

Eleanor nodded and proceeded to the kitchen at the back of the house. Along the way Eleanor noticed how neat and tidy everything was. With a house this small it doesn't take much for it to look unkept but everything was in its place and this impressed Eleanor. Either she is a fabulous housekeeper, or she readied her place for Eleanor's arrival. Somehow, Eleanor believed it was the latter.

Eleanor seated herself at a chair at the kitchen table and waited for Anne's mother to be seated. She poured them both a cup of coffee and presented sugar and creamer to which Eleanor accepted and prepared her coffee. Then Eleanor said, "I am sure you are wondering why I am here this morning." And Candice nodded, agreeing that she was indeed wondering.

"I am not going to beat around the bush and will just come out with it. You see Candice, I have been investigating a rumor I heard that your daughter Anne would be sister to my best friend Bella Thomas. I found that so hard to believe that Bella's father could do that to his family. Then I thought I had to find out for sure so, I made some arrangements to get some DNA from Anne and Bella's father and without their knowledge, ran a paternity test. Before I proceed any further, I want to ask you if you know anything about this?" said Eleanor as she stared directly at Anne's mother.

The woman was in shock. Her heart was racing, and she found it hard to breath. How could this story be out there and how did Eleanor Becks find out about this? She didn't know what to say or even how to answer this. She began with a whispered…" I am not sure what you are talking about Ms Becks. What has this kind of information have to do with me anyway?" she added.

"Let me see if I can explain this to you clearly and then I am going to ask you again if you can clear this up for me, okay with you?" stated Eleanor sternly.

"You see, most everyone in town can agree that your daughter looks a great deal like Bella Thomas and then someone came to me and said that Bella's father had an affair with someone he worked with at the factory and that Anne was indeed Bella's sister from her father's infidelity," said Eleanor. "Since you are Anne's mother it stands to reason that you were that woman at the factory that Charlie, Bella's father probably had an affair with. Now is that a fact or not?" asked Eleanor.

Anne's mother sat calmly as she tried desperately to think about how she was going to answer this question. "I really don't have to answer your question Ms Becks. My life is none of your business and I am going to ask you to leave my house now if you would please. I have things I need to do." Said a very shaky woman trying to not show that she was unnerved.

Eleanor was not budging and was not going to leave without an answer to her questions. She was hell bent on making this woman come clean on her participation in this charade. Eleanor really wanted to know why she would do this to anyone.

"I am going to sit here until you give me an answer to my question. Or you can call the sheriff if you wish. I am sure he would be most interested in your answer as well," stated Eleanor. Eleanor crossed her arms across her chest and stared straight into the eyes of Anne's mother.

"My life is none of your business Ms Becks and I don't know why this is of any concern to you," she stated.

Eleanor sat up in her chair and stiffened her back and bellowed..." Because it affects my best friend and I won't have her hurt in any way."

Eleanor continued..." I believe the answer to my question is yes. That you are the woman Bella's father had an affair with. Did you indeed get pregnant by Charlie," asked Eleanor, watching for any trace of response? With that question she could see that Anne's mother was starting to shake and getting very edgy.

"Well, if you must know; yes. I did have an affair with Charlie. He and I have been friends for many years and a long time ago we got a little carried away and we both regretted that. We kept it quiet for the sake of his family and not until his wife recently passed away; did we rekindle our relationship. This is, however, nobody's business but ours. We didn't hurt anyone and we don't want this information about town." She added.

Eleanor just stared at her and then asked her..." Does Anne believe that Charlie is her father?" And, with that question, Anne's mother got very defensive.

"What difference does that make?" She blared out. "Stay out of my daughter's business and leave her alone. She had to grow up without a father and possibly now she can have one if you leave her alone." Eleanor just stared in disbelief at what this woman was saying.

"It is obvious to me that by your reaction to my question that Anne does believe that Charlie is her father," said Eleanor.

Candice says, "What if she does. What has that got to do with you or Bella?"

"What if Charlie was NOT Anne's father after all?" Said Eleanor. Anne's mother looked shocked.

"What are you talking about?" Candice asked.

With that Eleanor explained that the paternity test proved that Charlie was not Anne's father. Eleanor explained that she had obtained DNA from Charlie and Anne and had them tested at the lab in town and the test came back negative of being related to one another.

Anne's mother collapsed into a kitchen chair in shock. It was obvious to Eleanor that she had no idea that Charlie was not the father. Had she been wrong all these years? Her mind was racing. She had told Anne that Charlie was her father and watched her daughter be so angry at this man and he wasn't the one she should have been mad at. This is unbelievable! What has she done?

Eleanor got up and walked out of the house. She had her answer. It was apparent that this woman had no idea who Anne's real father was. She had perpetuated a lie that is causing some serious damage to many people.

Things were about to get ugly for David and Anne both and who knows what the future will hold for Bella and her relationship with her father. Everything is about to come unglued and life will never be the same.

David and Anne had breakfast brought to her hotel room. They just lounged around most of the morning.

David told Anne that they didn't need to go to the bank until around lunch time as that was when the major administrative people would be away for lunch and that she should be able to march right in there with him as if she were Bella. This way she could sign a signature card as Anne Thomas and nobody would suspect a thing. This could be just like when they bought the house and the land in Nassau the last time they were there.

Anne was getting excited to get things moving and she kept checking the time. She thought she would hear from her mother this morning, but she hadn't heard anything yet. She had to learn to be patient. All good things come with time and she knew it was about to be the best day of her life. Everything she ever wanted was just about ready to happen. Her heart was flipping with excitement and she had to pinch herself a couple of times as she knew this was the day that would change the rest of her life.

Finally, at 11:30 David said that they needed to get going. Both were dressed and ready to leave. They hailed a cab and headed to the bank. They expected to arrive around 12:05 which, in David's mind was perfect as most of the managers would be headed out or already gone to lunch.

On the ride over to the bank David began to feel something very odd. He thought they were being followed and the cab driver assured him they were not. The uneasiness did not go away.

They arrived at the bank at exactly 12:05 and walked slowly through the front door. David approached the receptionist and stated his business. He wished to speak to the bank manager to arrange for his wife to sign signature cards on his account. Additionally that he also had some transfers coming in that he needed to verify. The receptionist requested that they be seated while she finds someone to help them. She left her desk and disappeared down the hallway.

David & Anne sat down and waited. David observed that the bank lobby was pretty much empty which seemed odd to him.

A different woman came back to the desk and approached David saying that one of her managers could help him and would they please follow her to that office. David took Anne's hand, and they followed this woman to an office that was at the end of the hallway.

They went inside the office and sat down. The woman said the manager would be there shortly to assist them and then she left closing the door behind her.

A big burly kind of man came through the office door and sat down behind the desk. He introduced himself and David had to ask him to repeat his name as he said it very fast.

"Nice to meet you Carlos", said David trying to be friendly. "We won't take too much of your time. Here is my bank account number and I need you to verify that some prearranged transfers have happened this morning and then I also need to get my wife here on the account so she will need to sign a signature card. Can you take care of these things for us?" David asked Carlos.

"Most certainly sir. That is what I do", said Carlos with a matter-of-fact tone. He turned and went to the computer on his desk and entered information and then David's account number asking David to input his password on the account so he could verify the transfers. David entered the password in the computer.

"Mr. Thomas, there seems to be a hold on your account for some reason," stated Carlos. "It says that 11 million US dollars was transferred but it is being placed on a hold by the US Government." Then, another gentleman enters the room and asked David to please stand up and that he is being placed under arrest for trafficking funds outside of the United States jurisdiction and for embezzling other people's funds.

David starts to protest and another gentleman enters the room holding a gun pointed at David asking him to please turn around so the hand cuffs could be placed on his wrists. David complies and is dumb founded as he is not aware of how they know about his plan.

Carol Johnson steps into the room and introduces herself to David, who is now handcuffed and to Anne who is sitting in the room in shock as to what is going on. She is staring at David trying to ask what is happening with her eyes.

Carol says…"Mrs. Thomas, will you please step over here for a moment and provide me with proof of your identity please." And she escorts Anne over to a corner of the room. Anne looks at David and then at Carol and is unsure what to do next.

"Mrs. Thomas, your identification please," insists Carol. Anne just looks at her and starts to go into her purse to pull out her identity then stops as she realizes what is happening. She has been impersonating someone else and didn't have the right identification and was now in trouble herself.

Carol turns Anne around and pulls her arms behind her back and tells her … "Ms. whomever you are, you are now under arrest for impersonating someone you are not for the sake of embezzling funds with Mr. Thomas here." stated Carol very clearly as she places Anne's wrists into the handcuffs. Both David and Anne were provided their Miranda Rights and then escorted out of the bank into the police cars that were sitting outside of the bank and taken directly to the police department a few blocks away.

Yes indeed. Life has changed from this moment forward and not where Anne thought it was going to end up.

CHAPTER 9

The Conclusion

The regroup meeting was scheduled for 8:00 pm and everyone was present including the 2 assistants in the meeting room. Everyone fixed themselves a beverage and was just chatting before they could begin their meeting.

In a few moments Eleanor motioned for everyone to move to their meeting room where they were robed and proceeded with their opening ritual. This process never changed and kept them on track. Once all the candles were lit and the chants uttered, they were seated in their respective chairs and waited for Eleanor to begin.

"Welcome everyone. I am glad you are here; and we miss our Bella. But, as you know, she cannot be present during this portion of our meeting. Let me bring you all up to speed as to where we are at this moment," said Eleanor as she began the meeting.

"At approximately 11:30 this morning I received a telephone call from Nassau, Bahamas that David Thomas and Anne Bellgrath have been arrested by the OIG (Office of Inspector General) for embezzlement and for impersonating another individual without their approval. They were processed through the OIG and then on to the FBI channels and were extradited back to the United States and now sit in jail cells in Washington, DC. It is with great pleasure that I advise you that they won't be seen for a very long time as the OIG and FBI have plenty of evidence to put them away for a very long time. David will more than likely also have to face charges in Spain as his visa records were modified illegally and they are requesting that he be brought back to Madrid for charges to be brought against him there. This will be reviewed by our State Dept.

The sisters all gave out a large sigh of relief and then Evie asked Eleanor, "What about Anne being Bella's sister. That has kept me awake for 3 days now."

Eleanor offers…" Not an issue on that count. I had a long conversation with Candice, Anne's mother today and it seems that she always thought that Bella's father Charlie was Anne's father when in fact a paternity test done on DNA samples from Anne and Charlie prove that they are not related." explains Eleanor.

"I believe that she was in shock when I left her home this morning and I sincerely believe that she had no idea that Charlie was not Anne's father," says Eleanor.

This poor woman has now lost her daughter because of her uninformed statements. Charlie has not been told yet as I am sure that he still thinks he is Anne's father. I will make sure he knows the truth later," she states.

"Looks like our issue with David and Anne is corrected. Now we must be strong to help Bella through this process," said Eleanor.

"We must get some additional paperwork corrected as David bought some real estate in Nassau and had Anne sign as Anne Thomas on the documents. We need to get these transactions reversed or corrected. This will take some doing but it can be done," said Eleanor as everyone nodded in agreement.

"I can help with part of that and so can Luna," stated Evie. "I have experience in real estate transactions and can work with the people in Nassau to make this happen. They just need to speak with Bella as to how she wants to handle the paperwork. She can either resell the property or keep it with proper name changes, etc." explains Evie.

Luna asks… "What about the money that David supposedly transferred to Nassau that belonged to Bella. What happened with that?"

Eleanor quickly added, "We got that money transferred back to a new account for Bella yesterday before David knew that it was transferred out. We knew he was planning on embezzling money from his business to the Nassau account so we made sure Bella's money was out of that account before the OIG and FBI got there and froze the funds. Her money is safe with us now and she will be okay financially," added Eleanor.

"I am so happy about that. Lord knows that poor girl worked hard for that money and it would have been horrible for her to lose it to that idiot," added Luna.

And the sisters all agreed.

"Together we stand. We will continue to help Bella and see her through this nightmare and to keep this information within our sisterhood. Nobody is to speak of this situation outside of our walls and let's continue our diligence to safely protect and look out for one another," Eleanor stated and they all nodded in agreement.

PREVIEW - BOOK 2 - ELEANOR
Chapter 1

Bella arrived home the next day to find her home in a bit of an upheaval as some OIG people had been in her home and turned everything upside down. Claudette was working hard with the other household staffers to get things back together when Bella walked through the front door. Claudette ran to meet her and grabbed her suitcase immediately and gave her a gentle hug welcoming her home.

She looked at Bella and saw the grief on her face and said…"no worries Ms. Bella. Everything has been taken care of and you are now home safe and sound. Let's get you upstairs and unpacked so you can relax," said Claudette and she helped Bella up the stairs to get her unpacked.

Bella allowed Claudette to help her up the stairs to her bedroom. She is tired but happy to be home. She is looking forward to a long conversation with Eleanor.

High up in the sky on a supersonic jet flies Hector, returning to Barcelona, Spain to bring new information to Mr. Delgado regarding David Thomas. Mr. Delgado will not be happy.